ROADSIDE MIDNIGHT

Boris B. Blinkov

First edition
Released July 2024
0% AI assisted
0% AI generated
Written, edited and illustrated by Boris

to H
to M

Part 1 - Bus stop

I look up.

The cold spring rain falls on my face as I get off the stuffy inner-city bus. It was another uneventful workday. I am now just a five minute walk from home. A quick snack sausage and a cold beer from gas station and I'm finally home. Exhaustion washes over me like relief after a day of work in the potato field. Stressful and thoroughly relaxing at same time. But I am not a field worker. I work in the office. And I am simply tired from the neck up. "No more brain today" I think to myself as I stare into the grey distance of apartment buildings and muster up the willpower to start walking. Before I can take two steps in the right direction, I hear my name called out. "Lev! LEV!"

I look around. To my surprise, I see my younger cousin, Alex, in his usual silver station wagon. He is stopped at a red light at the intersection right next to me, in the opposite lane of my bus stop, gesturing aggressively to get in the car, a wide smile on his face of pure excitement. I look at him, slightly puzzled. His light turns green. He whips his head around, does a quick u-turn, driving his front tire over the curb, almost crashing into the lamp post as everyone takes a cautionary step back. A cloud of diesel smoke follows him as per tradition at this point, as he stops right in front of me, throws open his passenger side door and excitedly yells "GET IN!"

At this point, I don't need to think about "why?" or ask redundant questions like "what are you doing here?" When an opportunity like this arises, you just go. We're close. We've been close since birth. I don't even stop to wonder why he's driving around this area, especially since he lives five kilometres away. He drives almost everywhere. All the time. For anything. How he manages to stay fit being glued to a car seat like that amazes me to this day. I take my work bag from my shoulder, throw it in the back seat and jump in the car, just as the bus that has appeared behind us starts honking its horn and its driver gestures to us that we both have brain damage. I give the bus driver a congratulatory thumbs up and close the passenger door. I give a quick handshake to Alex as we accelerate away, leaving the bus, the bus stop and everyone in it in a thick cloud of diesel smoke. This sight of a thick black cloud of exhaust fumes is completely comedical which I admire from the side mirror. I blast the stereo on loud and realise that it wasn't the thumb I was showing the bus driver. Oh well. Such is life in the city.

I rest my head back, take a deep breath, look up through the partially fogged up sunroof and suddenly realise exactly what I need to do. A clear path manifests in my mind. A plan, a goal. It feels like it's what I have always wanted. It feels as if it's the only thing I have ever wanted in my life. I tell Alex "you know what? Let's just go." He looks at me and nods. He understands. No explanation, he already knows.

"Thought you'd never say. Let's go," he replies with pure excitement. "Let's stop by my place first."

Without hesitation he pushes the gas pedal to the floor and the whistling turbo under the hood pushes the engine to fly us faster toward where we will end up. We are on our way.

PINES. Yes. Pines and junipers are all that I want to smell right now, not diesel smoke. And not the junipers crushed into a bottle of gin, although that potion has recently brought more solace to me than I dare to admit out loud. I could fall asleep right now between the aromatic bushes of wild juniper and wake up as new person with clear mind twelve hours later. Complete peace. I would probably need a tent though. The weather is rough.

It's a Monday.

Part 2 - Concrete palace

The excitement of the unknown washes over me like a warm summer wave from the hot evening sea. There's something utterly profound about taking a long step toward a goal you know might not exist. It's what drives us. You can plan something to the finest detail, but in the end it always unfolds in a completely unique way, out of our control.

We drive through the midtown railroad crossing that divides the newly rebuilt part of the city from the seemingly forgotten. In a few minutes we arrive at Alex's place - a 16 storey high-rise apartment building from the 1970s. He, however, lives on the first floor.

The courtyard in front of the building is filled to the absolute fucking brim with parked cars. Some on street, some on grass, some on sidewalk. Nevertheless he manages to find a suitable spot, although blocking off a few parked cars while doing so.

"Is ok, I know them. They not home" he says with certainty. "Besides, I only need 3 minutes, and then, boom, we go."

I look at the blocked off cars, shrug and reply "eh, what they going to do anyway? Block you back? Hah!"

I swing open the passenger door, creaking louder than a church basement hatch, and step outside. The weather has remained surprisingly the same, small drops of cold spring rain through a seemingly endless cover of clouds. I am actually more surprised that it doesn't rain all the time.

"This weather is absolute fucking comedy, one day rain, other day more rain. Might as well move to babushka's basement, there's same amount of sun there" I say.

"No no no, rain good news, mean more crops for harvest" Alex replies as he reaches in his pocket and lights a cigarette.

"What crops, you live in apartment building and work in construction. What fucking crops are you harvesting? Also, it's spring. Only thing that grows now is debt and depression."

"Did I not tell you? I found abandoned plot near the old kolkhoz back in Bardok. Plant seed, see what grow" he says with mild excitement.

"Wait. You went back? When?" I ask with genuine curiosity.

Bardok used to be an infamous small town for hosting underground rave parties in the abandoned kolkhoz buildings some years ago. The town locals never seemed to mind, but still the events suddenly stopped two years ago. No one knew where the organisers came from, or where they went, or even who they really were. It was an open secret that these events even happened. Most who went, denied their existence, others praised the great organising skills of the anonymous party masters. Either way, an aura of enigma loomed over it all.

Alex puts out his cigarette, inhales a big lungful of city air and replies with a clear sense of victory "I didn't just go back. I found something. Something you need to see. Let's stop by there, is only 30 minute detour from our destination."

"Man, I don't care if it's a three *hour* detour, I want to see what happened to that site," I reply as I grab my work bag from the back seat and head to the apartment with Alex.

Alex is exactly three months younger than me, but constantly tries to prove he is more grown up. I bought car, he bought bigger car. I stopped wearing trackpants to work, he started going to work in suit. I got promoted to manager of recruitment... he bought an even bigger car. His apartment is a two room rental in the lower class part of town. He moved here when he first got started at his current job three years ago, and hasn't moved since. According to his words, he likes being close to his clients' levels of accommodation and not boost his status higher by moving. I completely agree with his desire to be similar to the people he works for, but I'm not sure if a first storey apartment across the street from a pawn shop and shady casino is the ideal place to live, especially considering he keeps his tools in the car. Alex is very much an I-deal-with-it-when-it-happens type of person, meaning he won't spend a cent on improving his life unless completely necessary. I admit, I highly envy this side of his personality.

Also, he's always had a thing for practical cars even though he lives alone and never carries more than a box of work equipment. But I never question his ambitions and neither does he mine.

The old soviet-era apartment buildings have always reinforced my belief that the world changes slowly, and only slowly. At least around this part of the world. The effort it would take to one day get the resident's consent to move them out and demolish this massive high-density concrete palace is unmeasurable. But this would only occur if the building was on the verge of collapse, and this behemoth still looks like it will stand 60 more years without any noticeable degradation.

We step inside the building. The dimly lit hallways always smell like a mix of mould and wet dogs. Staircases are exactly so wide as to fit a coffin through. Elevators, which were mandatory for all buildings with more than five storeys, are slow, loud and look like they would come crashing down after each use. But they never do. They were built to last, as was everything and everyone else at the time.

My satirical admiration of this Soviet palace is interrupted by Alex, who takes a large bunch of keys out of his pocket, picks a single key attached to a small metal keyholder in the shape of Eiffel tower, operates the massive metal doors with a series of clangs and opens the path to his glorious Soviet apartment. I step inside, throw my bag on the couch, click the radio on and sit down. It never ceases to amaze me how the interior of most of these '70s apartments look exactly the same. And for good reason, too. With one colour of wallpaper and two shades of linoleum for the kitchen floor to choose from, you had to get creative with other things instead, like where to place the potted plants that you eventually end up getting to not go crazy. Most people had an onion or two growing on the windowsill as well. Alex was no different, although his other indoor plants had long died shortly after he moved in. I'm sure the landlord wouldn't miss them.

A loud bang and the sound of someone wrestling a bear come from the kitchen. Suddenly Alex appears in the doorway with two bottles - one beer and one kvass. He sends the bottle of beer flying toward me and says "I'm driving. You stay hydrated." I catch the bottle, which almost misses me and nearly hits the nearby massive painted radiator, grab the apartment key from the table, equip the Eiffel tower shaped keyholder and pop open the drink. The beer is cold, cold enough to reverse global warming for a week. I take a small sip.

"Where you import this from, the fucking Ural mountains?" I ask him. "I get brain freeze just from smelling this thing".

Alex appears from kitchen with what seems like a feast for three people - eggs, bread, sausages, coffee, and the previously seen bottle of kvass.

"Ey, what is refrigerator for if not make thing cold? I want half-warm drink I put on balcony, but coldbox is for cold," he replies and proceeds to demolish the plate of food in under a minute.

"Shit, man, that's some expert military training right there" I say with visible impression "you even feel taste of any of that?"

"Taste? Not time for taste. You start enjoying taste of food too much, you get big and fat. Food is for keeping alive, keep strong until next food arrive" he replies as he finishes the last piece of bread on his plate.

"You know what? We should get in touch with the original organisers of that Bardok rave" I say as I take another sip from the beer. "I wonder why the blin they ever stopped. I could use a good party right now."

"Yeah, good luck. We have more chance of finding gold in sewage system," Alex replies, wiping his mouth clean with his sleeve. "They probably got shut down by police, local mafia or both. Let's just send message to whole contact list, we have party even bigger at my place in 30 minutes."

There is a fascinating phenomenon about us. We both realised very early in our lives that when we're hanging around together, people flock to us like seagulls at a fish market. It was unstoppable. At first it seemed odd, especially knowing that most anyone of these people would never talk to either of us individually, but as a two man group we were the main attraction. If either of us ever felt bored, we simply had to meet up and people would just gather out of the woodwork like ants. I remember many times never even mentioning us having any plans together, but as we met up, someone was surely to write, call or walk up to ask what we are up to. Yes, we. Never either of us separately. Very odd, yet completely the norm for us. Maybe because we were close like brothers. Maybe because people saw us as a two man act. In any case, when either of us was bored, all we had to do was meet up and the adventure would form around us. I had a feeling today was no different.

I chug what's left of my beer, grab my bag and start heading out. Alex follows, grabbing a toothbrush along the way. I step outside and suddenly the weather has changed from a depressing spring overcast to a sunny day of May. This is a sign. I completely forget the fact that it's a workday tomorrow and start planning my escape from the city. "We should take Karloff street, avoid the traffic."

"Hah! What traffic? Everyone already at home sleeping. Only people driving on Monday out of city are bus drivers and immigrants."

"So what does that make us?"

"That? That makes us the smart ones. Let's go!"

He clicks open his car door but then suddenly pauses in his tracks. He spots a person on the balcony right next to us. I recognise the figure, it is Filip. He looks slightly happier than usual, uncharacteristic even. He's smiling, smoking, looking down at the street level where we are. He gives a quick nod in our direction.

"What you happy about, payday come early?" I ask the strangely happy man on the second storey balcony.

"Car sold today. Let's go celebrate, I'm buying," he replies, ready to hit the bar at a moment's notice.

I take a quick look around. "Oh yeah, the rust content of the parking lot has decreased significantly. How much did you get for the old '05?"

"Fuck you Lev, we all know you couldn't afford it. How's the bus schedule, huh? Still riding with bums to city and back?"

"Hah! The only bum I see is screaming out of his balcony smoking black market cigarettes," I quickly reply.

A silence follows. Then a longer silence. Suddenly, we all laugh. I swear I hear people laughing on street, too.

"So what you say? My money no good for you city kids?" asks the brush cut, skinny, tracksuit wearing gopnik in the window.

Filip used to go to same school as us, but instead of graduating, he got a summer job and never quit. He was a year above us, but always sounded like he could be our grandfather. Probably because he was brought up mostly by his grandparents. He is, at this point, the only one of us who has gotten married. The biggest mistake of his whole adult life, as he had repeatedly told us over a glass or two of vodka.

I look at Alex, he looks back at me and says "eeeeeey, you buy first round, we always ready for action."

Filip takes quick look inside the apartment, steps in, emerges seconds later with a half bottle of brandy in his hand. Grabs the pack of cigarettes and lighter from the balcony into other and steps on the ledge. In one smooth motion, he drops from the balcony, lands on feet on the small patch of grass under his window, does a roll on the ground and stands up, as if he's practised it for years.

Filip gets in the car. "Sorry patsans, I could not get to freezer with vodka, wife cooking in kitchen."

"Won't she be mad you left without saying anything?" I ask.

"Only if she finds out. Besides, that's nothing. Just wait 'til she realise I took the only set of home keys. Davai, comrades, life is short. Let's not extend it by wasting time. Let's hit the bar" he says muffled, as he pulls out a wad of cash, while a half smoked cigarette hangs from his mouth. He uncorks the brandy and takes a swig.

Alex starts up the car, shifts it into gear and manoeuvres out from the maze of cars. We are on our way.

Part 3 - The Red Dog

The sun arrives in the day like an unexpected guest to a house party. But instead of a stingy friend from down the street, this guest is more like a hot girl who brought a case of cold beer and bottle of vodka. We are all completely stunned by the weather change. Especially Alex, whose driving has deteriorated from his usual "fluid" style to an even more dangerous one. Luckily the little traffic there is clears out as we drive further from the residential area. It takes no more than 15 minutes for us to drive to the city centre. As the time is nearing 6PM, there is no problem finding a parking spot in midtown as everyone working in the city has left for home. Alex parks the car, turns off the engine and announces "end of line, everyone out!"

"One quick drink, and we're off. We going to Volkonsk" I say as we get out of the parked car.

"What TODAY? Fuck that, I want some of this action too" Filip suddenly screams, as if waking from a deep sleep.

I look at Alex, he gives a quick look back with a smirk on his face. "Davai. You pay for fuel and you can come along" he tells Filip and opens the door to the pub.

"Oooooy you fucking hagglers. One tank of fuel, no more. But you buying my boat ticket. I still have funeral cost to cover once wife finds out I left without saying where."

Filip had lost his phone a few weeks ago after a night on the town. Considering his track record with booze, I wouldn't be surprised if it fell out of his pocket. He still adamantly believes it was stolen from him at the very moment he turned his back to take a leak next to the old town park statue. It was no surprise he wanted to tag along for the trip, as his life had become exponentially more stale after he lost his job a few weeks ago. But honestly, who wouldn't want to come along to Volkonsk island, beautiful nature, surrounding sea to dip into. People who go, always seem to be happy just to be there. It's paradise. We enter the pub and sit down at our regular table.

"I'd kill for some good shashlik right now. None of this oil-washed pub food" I say looking at the menu.

"Really? Who?" Alex asks, looking at his menu.

"What?"

"Who would you kill for some good shashlik?"

"*Who*? In this economy? Nobody. But put me in a room with a hunting knife and a pig and we all eating tonight. I'm fucking starving."

Just at that moment, the waitress comes over, seemingly appearing out of thin air.

"Some oil-washed bread and potatoes for you gentlemen? Or would you like I bring whole pig instead?" she asks as she looks at me with genuine curiosity.

"Let's start with three beers, three vodkas and the usual plate of sausage, our good friend comrade Filip is paying today. We will work up the appetite for the pig as we go along, thank you Masha."

"So, Lev, you still longing for that country lady or you back to talking to us city girls?" Masha curiously asks as she writes down our order.

"Don't worry about me, I moved on fast once I heard what she did."

"You mean *who*, she did, am I right? Or more like who *didn't* she do!" Alex screams across the table, laughing.

"Well, you let me know how I can help" Masha says, as she rips a small piece of paper from her order flipbook and hands it to me, then goes to the bar to fix our drinks.

"Seriously? How? What fucking pimp were you in past life to have skill like this?" Filip asks, as he looks at the piece of paper with Masha's phone number on it. "I couldn't get laid in a whorehouse if the world was ending. You didn't even have to say anything."

"Maybe if you stopped expecting the world to end someone would actually be interested. Also, you're married. Don't you get enough action at home?" I ask him.

"Oh you simple man, you don't get married to get more action, you get married to make the action stop. You pay bills and wait for death to come. Then down a few bottles of vodka to make the suffering go faster," Filip says as he looks toward the bar, waiting for drinks to arrive.

Some people step into the pub, then even more briefly follow. A rare sight for a Monday, but nothing impossible considering the bland time of year. There's not much to do besides work and sleep in this city, anyway. The bar, simply called The Red Dog, is situated away from main roads and tourist attractions. Realistically you would not expect this place to get as much traffic as it does, considering its poor location, but here we are, looking as it fills up with more and more people, this dimly lit cave of booze and scratched up wooden tables. Decorated liberally with what look like Christmas lights running across the ceiling, shining above as their reflection shimmers on the bar full of cocktail glasses and beer jugs. The Red Dog is situated on the edge of old town, near the freight train tracks. I briefly ponder the great financial benefit of owning a bar in a city full of semi-professional alcoholics, but get interrupted by the arrival of the waitress with our refreshments. Alex and Filip are engaged in what seems like a heated argument about the benefits of car ownership, but I barely understand a word as I'm completely zoned out.

"You really need to stop eavesdropping on us, it is very impolite. We could be talking about secret undercover mission plans here," I say as Masha places our drinks in front of us.

"Then maybe you want to keep your undercover operations more quiet," Masha replies. "Even the kitchen staff can hear what you talking about. Actually, the group two tables away just asked me a very strange question. Were you just talking about The White Hornet?"

We all three look at her in confusion as if she quoted ancient Greek scripture.

"We were just talking about Filip's old beaten down Lada 2105" Alex replies and points toward Filip with his beer glass.

"Fuck you *beaten down,* my car drives smoother than your shitbucket" Filip quickly retaliates. "You got more rust than junkyard after a rainy day."

"Eyyyy few coats of paint and my Silver Shadow rides to see another day" Alex replies. "Also, last I checked, you traded your car for few shots of ice cold vodka. Cheers friends!" Alex raises the shot of vodka from the table, looks at the group two tables down, yells "here's to you" and takes the shot.

"You been *sniffing* that paint or what? Rust has become central part of your car's structure. We crash into post, one half roll east, other part west" Filip replies and takes his shot and they continue arguing.

I turn to the waitress. "Excuse the neanderthals at my table, who's The White Hornet?"

"Not a *who*, it's a car. White 2105, white rims, black roof, blue decals on side," Masha clarifies.

"Lowered, with a small spoiler on the trunk? Pretty beaten up paint job?" I ask her.

"Yeah, so you know it."

"Well, either someone has copied your car, Filip, or she is actually talking about your '05." I say looking at Filip sitting next to me, visibly shocked at the new information. "I didn't realise it had a name. Who gave it that?"

"I thought everyone knew. Vova. You know, Mostovich," Masha replies.

"VOVA THE FUCKING RACING DRIVER?" I yell, almost tipping over my beer. "Blyaaaaat, Filip! No no no no." Filip has fallen down onto the table, holding on to his head in disbelief of what he has done. "How did you not know about this? How much did you sell it for? That shit is worth a fortune to right buyer!" I say with massive grin on my face.

A small voice from the direction of Filip says "less than a fortune. Less for what I bought it for."

Me and Alex burst out laughing. Masha is trying to hold back her laughter and walks back to the bar to deal with the new clients that just stepped in.

"Do you at least know who you sold it to?" Alex asks. "You sure it wasn't Vova? That would be fucking amazing" he says and starts laughing.

Filip raises his head from the table to take a sip of his beer. "No no it was some woman. Sasha or Sofia or something" and places his head back on the table.

"Do we know any Sashas or Sofias that would be crazy enough to drive a Lada?" Alex replies. "Also, how did we not notice that Filip was driving a fucking racing driver's tuned up '05?"

"Well, Filip drives like a babushka most of the time anyway" I reply. "Only time I was ever in that car, we were stalling in rush hour traffic. Yes the exhaust was loud but I assumed Filip had applied the hole punch tuning to it. How did it run? Any better performance than other Ladas?"

"Well, yes it drove smoother than other '05s but I assumed that was because it was well maintained. The paint job was good, didn't drink oil…"

"I won't argue with that. Most cars I've seen you buy are ass," Alex says.

Filip waves his hand at Alex dismissively and places head back on table, contemplating having made the biggest mistake of his life.

"But the fact that a '05 didn't need maintenance should have been a massive red flag itself." Alex replies. "How many kilometres did you run with it?"

Filip raises two fingers.

"Two thousand?" Alex says nearly screaming. Filip shakes his head and waves his two raised fingers around more aggressively. "TWENTY THOUSAND? With no maintenance?" Alex bursts out laughing. "Two more rounds of vodka to this table! I'm buying."

"But wait, this would mean the last seller didn't know what he had. Maybe the new buyer doesn't know either," I say. "Maybe you could buy it back."

"I doubt it" Masha says, suddenly having appeared with six shots of vodka. "Sonya bought it."

"I don't know a Sonya" Alex says. "Not in this city anyway. Who is she? What does she do?"

"She runs that small booze business in the city. Imports exclusive drinks to the country. Comes by here once a week, talks business with the manager," Masha says as she cleans up some empty glasses from our table. "She was here today with that car. Parked outside, exactly where your car is now. Probably was showing it off to the locals."

"Well pizdec, Filip!" I say as I raise a glass. "Here's to you and your track record with cars… and women!"

We all raise our glasses, take the shots and finish the rest of the beers and snacks. Shortly after I realise we no longer have a sober driver to take us to Bardok, not to mention Volkonsk. Since none of us have any wish to go back home, then getting to where we need to go is the only real solution.

The vision of junipers, pines and sleeping among them slowly starts to dissolve from my head, being replaced with a much more likely scenario of arriving at home, dropping into bed and falling asleep completely intoxicated.

"FUCK!" I scream and smash my fist on the table with such force that makes the glasses jump up from the table. "I'm going to Volkonsk one way or another." I stand up, walk to the bar and address the whole pub from there. "I need a ride to Volkonsk island. Today. Preferably with a stop at Bardok. I carry two patsans with me, ready to pay for fuel. Who is up for the challenge?"

Silence. Well, shit. Getting a ride out of town on a Monday was probably too hopeful anyway. I turn to the bar, ready to make one last order. Some drinks for the road. Might as well take the bus. Before I can start putting my request into words, the pub door behind me falls open, the evening sun shining into the dark room like a bright set of full beam headlights in my face during a midnight drive. I turn to see the cause of this inconvenience as I mutter "cyka" under my breath. I quickly freeze for a moment as I stand in disbelief of what has appeared in the doorway along with the gleaming sun. A beautiful young woman, holding a case of beer and a four-pack of vodka on top of it. I am utterly stunned as she looks into the pub, coming from the outside we must look like molemen to her.

"Excuse me, you know you're not supposed to *bring* the drinks. They provide the drinks here" I tell her as I watch her place the boxes on the counter.

"Oh hi" she says with a surprise on her face. "Oh I just thought a little extra won't hurt. You know, just in case they run out." She goes back out and returns with another few cases of beer.

"There a party starting? What did I miss?" I ask with visible confusion. "You got many more of those coming? Let me give you a hand."

"Sure, you look like you can handle the really heavy stuff," she replies, hinting at my intoxication and leads the way outside, showing signs of exhaustion.

I approach the exit of the pub and see Filip from the corner of my eye waving his hands and mouthing the words "WHAT THE FUCK! HOW?"

I step out of our favourite drinks establishment and I'm greeted by a hot wave of evening swelter. The first of the year. The blinding sun burns my eyes and blinds me for a brief moment. I take my time to adjust to the new environment. I'm now convinced - the summer has arrived early. My eyes get used to the brightness and I'm briefly in shock as I realise the girl I followed outside has disappeared. Was this a sign? Have I finally gone crazy? Has alcohol consumption finally burned my last brain cell and made me see things? Suddenly, for the second time today I hear my name being called out. "Lev. LEV!"

I turn left and there she is! Peeking around the corner from behind the building.

"You have me at a disadvantage. You know me, I don't know you," I say as I approach the edge of the building and stand there for a moment to chat.

"I've seen you perform," the girl quickly replies. "I recognised you immediately at the bar. Thanks for giving a hand, Lev. The weather tonight is brutal. I've probably made over 40 stops already."

"No problem. Wait, *you* listen to '99 below'?" I ask with visible confusion. "I guess I really shouldn't be surprised. But you're not really our target audience."

"Oh. And who would they be?" she asks with a slight hint of sarcasm mixed with genuine interest.

"Men. They would almost always be men."

We go around the building and arrive at the smaller parking area. The sight that greets me surprises me so suddenly it makes me stop in my tracks, crunching the gravel under my shoes. It's Vova's fucking '05 Lada.

"I don't believe it!" I say standing still, looking at the girl opening the trunk to a lowered white Lada 2105 and revealing a stack of more boxes of beer and vodka. "THAT'S THE CAR! That's Filip's car. That makes you Sonya."

"Well it's nice to be recognised by a celebrity. Have we met before?" she asks as she reaches into the trunk, bending over. I avert my eyes so that the sight of her skintight jeans doesn't melt my brain together with the help of the already hot fucking cheese wheel of a sun in the sky.

I walk toward the car to help her out. "No, the waitress mentioned that she saw you driving something called The White Hornet. I'm just putting two and two together. By the way, who calls a car like that? I always call my cars women's names. Olga, Oksana, Sasha."

"Actually Vova named it," she replies. "You must be following his career if you know about the car," she says with a slight glimmer of a smile on her face.

"Actually I don't follow anyone's career. I'm having trouble following my own. My idiot friend Filip just sold this car to you. I just called it his bucket of bolts."

"And you know Filip too. You are a real local celebrity" she says smiling, with what seems like genuine sarcasm. "It's hardly a bucket of bolts though. Vova spent half his career building it, other half racing it."

"You speak of Vova on first name basis. Do you know him personally?" I ask her.

"Not really, I've been to see him drive a few times, but never actually got a chance to share a word," she says as she hands me two cases of beer. "Also, he's been stone cold sober most of his life, so it's hard for our paths to really cross. No chance of finding him in a palace of virtue as The Red Dog" she says, looking at me as if she's finally found the first normal human being in her life. "You know, I think I've seen your every live performance. At least in this city" she replies and takes two small cases of vodka and skillfully slams closed the trunk in one smooth motion.

"That means you saw our performance of a lifetime we had at the sports hall last month."

"Sure. You mean the time you had to order security to keep more people from getting in?"

"No, that was the new small club behind old town. I mean the time we had to use the event organiser's amps and we blew them out while playing 'The Face To Face'. Then finished the set by switching to acoustic guitar and playing the rest without amps. Also the organiser threatened to not pay us if we didn't finish the set, so it worked out for all."

We walk back to the pub. I kick the door open with my foot looking like some kind of a superhero arriving at a dry city with the first drop of alcohol in years. We walk inside, place the drinks on the counter and she continues the conversation.

"It's amazing I've never seen you in here. Does that mean you're playing here tonight?"

"Playing? More like drinking until blacked out. Which are often the same thing. We're actually trying to get to Volkonsk with a stop in Bardok, but our driver got impulsively intoxicated so we're stranded here, looking for a ride. Also, I've never seen *you* in here either. And I come here a lot."

"I only come here to restock, I've never really sat down at the tables. I usually bring the stuff in from the back, though.

These cases are a gift from the manufacturer, a present from me to the manager for our good business. I'm betting he will take these home for his own consumption, or maybe halve the price and sell it to some of his regulars. Why are you going to Bardok?"

"My friend Alex there," I say as I point to the table where my slightly intoxicated friend and a now even more surprised Filip are sitting, who's now holding onto his head, "was our today's driver until some half an hour ago. Now I'm lucky if I can hitchhike my way there. Whatever happens, I'm getting there today. I need to leave the city. I'm so done with this smog filled rattling concrete jungle."

"I can take you" she swiftly replies. "I'm planning to stop by there this week with my friend anyway. Might as well go today. You will need to get a ride to Volkonsk from there, though."

"Stop by? In Badrok? Hah! Nobody just stops by there. It's been abandoned for years."

"Even more reason to go. Besides, I love to see how those party grounds look now after all that time."

"Alright, I won't argue with that" I tell the persistent Lada owner and ask her to give me a moment and meet us outside as I go walk to my friends.

"YOU ARE A GOD" Filip screams as I walk toward the table. "That's her! That's the woman who bought the '05. Don't tell me you got her number too."

"Number? No. But she did offer us a ride to Bardok. TODAY."

Alex and Filip stare at me as if I just single handedly invented the glorious skill of conversation. Alex looks at me, shrugs and replies "sounds good, let's go. I'm sure Filip would like to have one last encounter with his Yellow Wasp or what it's called."

"The White Hornet! And it was the best car I ever owned" Filip says, as he raises his beer glass, as if ready to make a toast to the whole pub.

"Comrade, ten minutes ago you didn't even know the name of the previous owner. Now you ready to preach it's the best thing you owned?" Alex says jokingly.

"Masha, put on my tab, we leaving for Bardok!" I say as I stand up.

"I thought your friend here offered to pay today" she replies from behind the counter.

"Oh, no, Masha" Alex says as he gets up from the table. "He's suffered enough for one day."

We all step outside, the sharp evening sun still burning us hotter than a shashlik grill. And the sight that welcomes us is something out of a dream. Tuned up 1980s Lada, our new friend next to it, waving at us to get in, a case of beer waiting in the back seat. The sun reflecting off the black roof, not a cloud in the sky and the pub left behind us like a memory of the distant past. This is our life now. We get in the car, each pop open a beer and say a quick cheer to our new driver. She saved our day. I quickly grab my work bag from Alex's car as I have a feeling we might not see it for a while.

We are, once again, on our way.

Part 4 - Kolkhoz

I admire the seemingly endless daylight as we drive through the evening. The perpetual cover of clouds that used to block the sky had made me completely forget that there's a thing called sunshine, as it had been virtually the same weather since the last day of summer the previous year.

Sonya just picked up her friend from the city and assigned her to drive the Lada, as she herself wanted to partake in the in-car festivities and bar services. Sonya's friend, a coworker from a previous company, she calls simply M. A rare sight to encounter her behind the wheel, as most people who drive these cars are old men with grey hair and not good looking young women. We sing some old time folk songs and I reluctantly sing along when Alex starts blasting my songs from the stereo. A short hour later, we arrive at the abandoned kolkhoz where just a few years ago the legendary parties were held. The sun, still stuck as if nailed high to the sky, shows no sign of going down.

"MY POTATOES" Alex yells at them a loud welcome out of the window as we pull into the kolkhoz courtyard. He jumps out and disappears into a small set of trees around the main building.

A kolkhoz used to be a form of collective farming in the Soviet era. This kolkhoz consisted of many massive buildings, barns and warehouses that were used for keeping animals and storing crops and hay. There are also some smaller buildings further away, along with many massive fields, which have now overgrown into what look like an endless sea of tall grass and wild crops. The parties that used to go on here transformed the whole, roughly 20 hectares of land, into a massive orchestrated rave paradise each time. Although thoroughly cleaned up, there are still some signs of the previous parties, even though the last one happened two years ago. Some remains of scaffolds, some decorations that seem to be left behind, a few banners here and there and printed leaflets hidden away by the wind that blew them around. There are clear signs everywhere that the whole event was organised, even though most partygoers boasted it being a random place where people just happened to gather, and just watch a party unfold. After the parties ended, nobody ever really came back here, since it was so far out of the way of the common path and main highways. Despite the massive attendance, Alex was one of the few that came back here to explore the abandoned site any further. He appears some time later, visibly dirtier but completely satisfied with his result.

"I am farmer" he announces across the courtyard. He invites us all to his little patch of land behind the main building. There are clear signs of work by someone who knows what they are doing. A small bordering fence has also been built around the plot, buckets for water are laying around, and even a small wheelbarrow, for what I assume is for carrying away the final product.

"Impressive. So when's harvest? Or will we be left hungering for potato salad this year too?" I ask the self-proclaimed farmer.

"You keep laughing, in few months I bring home free food straight from ground. Give me little more time and I running whole pig farm here."

"You don't think the owners will notice you coming here and using their whole farm to feed yourself and grow a whole army of pigs?"

"Hah! Notice by who? This place been abandoned for two years, probably more than that before it."

The place and surrounding areas are definitely visibly uninhabited - no lights, no cars, no fresh beaten paths. Just a vague gravel covered footpath that could be here from decades ago.

"Alright farmer boy, what's next then? Chickens? Wheat? Some sugar beets for making samogon at home?" I ask the clown that is happily boasting in front of everyone.

"You keep laughing, one day I will buy this place and start own farm for real," Alex replies. "Just need to wash off the party smell and clean up the scaffoldings." He approaches me and pulls me aside. "Remember I mentioned I found something? I went to see it, it's still here. You need to come check it out," he says, checking that the others don't notice what he's talking about.

We go around the corner of the main building, leaving others out of sight. Sonya and M walking around the smaller building near the courtyard and Filip sitting next to the car, ready to get going, enjoying his half bottle of brandy he grabbed from home just before making his daring escape. We come to a massive closed barn door with a fairly overgrown entrance. The door is on the short end of what looks like a 50 metre narrow low barn that seems to have been used for raising and housing pigs. Alex jumps over some tall grass and disappears behind the edge of the house. I wrestle the overgrown flora and follow him. I'm instantly greeted by a familiar sight - him scaling a high narrow window, trying to look in for something to loot. But in this case it's a run down barn instead of communal housing building in abandoned worn down part of our home city. Alex invites me to take a look inside. I arrange some old scattered bricks into a small stack and mount the temporary tower-shaped structure in an effort to view this long-awaited surprise that he wanted to show me for hours.

"Look at that, my friend. We hit the jackpot" Alex says quietly as he marvels at what he has found. The sight that appears is absolutely incredible.

"Is that..." I start my question.

"It is."

"It is… beautiful."

Appearing in the dark farm building, on the dirt floor and placed between some rusty farming equipment, is a 2 metre high stack of multiple cases of what seems like imported vodka. This 2 metre wide and 2 metre long cube of packaged booze shines from the abandoned barn like a miniature sun, so bright, so welcoming. The brilliant white packaging with vibrant colours in contrast with the dark dank background of the barn looks like it was spawned in directly from a video game.

"I want to try some" I say as I feel my eyes getting bigger every second I stare at this exceptional artefact.

"Try? Sure. Let's just teleport inside just as the massive case of booze has. Besides, I'm sure it's been here for years."

"So? Vodka never goes bad. You know this."

"Guessing from the bright colouring of the package, it's probably some sugar water with light vodka flavour. You know the ones I mean" Alex replies. "Those things keep for a year at best."

"And that's exactly what we going to find out. Let's go" I say as I climb down from the small window and start to look for a way inside.

"You sure we should be doing this?" Alex asks hesitantly.

"Blin, you the one who dragged me out to the bushes behind some broken ass warehouse in the late night. There's glass and rubble everywhere. I wouldn't be surprised if the building is ready to collapse, too. It's probably there from a previous party that someone just forgot about. You know how big the parties were. Let's claim it, maybe is part of a scavenger hunt."

"How does someone just lose a few pallets of booze?"

"I don't know. Maybe the forklift driver was drunk?" I say and we both start laughing. "Besides we just take few bottles or a case and leave rest here. Now, let's look for a way inside."

It takes us a good ten minutes of checking windows, other doors around the house and even the roof for an access point, but no luck. The main door has padlock and the narrow windows are too small to fit through. Alex offers to smash one of the bigger windows in, but that's like using the difficulty slider to lower the game's challenge - too easy. Finally we find a small hatch on the absolute other side of the 50 metre long building. We both squeeze through the hatch that looks like a small feeding trough for the animals that used to be housed inside.

"Smell that fresh air" Alex says as he takes a deep breath in. The air inside is still thick with the smell of farm animals that used to reside here years ago. The walls are black with dirt, the walls themselves built from what looks like natural stone and mortar. The inside of the building is one long continuous hallway, once used to house farm animals. Nature has already started to reclaim much the interior of the building, but the roof seems to be sturdy enough, at least to survive our brief visit. We wander through the long house, seeing the massive white cube in the distance. The little light that shines from the small windows from each side of the building, dimly lights our path. The evening sun outside has finally started to go down and now colours our way with a deep orange hue. We walk through deep dirt, looking at old rusty farming equipment hanging on both sides of our path. The narrow windows either no longer have glass panes on them or they never did - either way we appreciate the fresh breeze that has aired out this barn for years. The rows of lights hanging from the ceiling remind me of the Christmas bulbs that decorate the interior of The Red Dog. Although the illumination in this building has stopped working long before we ever arrived. A sense of unease comes over us as we progress further down the seemingly endless hall of low ceilings and small wooden dividers used to keep pigs. It's quiet here. The outside sound of wind and birdsong is blocked out almost completely by the thick walls and narrow windows. After what seems like a 10 minute walk, we arrive at the room with the massive bright case of booze. The walls here are covered in ancient looking farm tools fit to furnish a museum. But that is not what interests us. We both cheer as we each start exploring a side of the massive case. Alex rips open the plastic wrapping on one edge, unpacks the bright packaging and checks the bottle.

"Hah! Expires in two years. Might as well be next century. Bottoms up!" he says as he throws me one and picks another from the box. Alex unscrews one and takes a few sips "you were right, Lev. As always. This was definitely worth it."

Before I sample the loot we have just come across, I take a minute to investigate further, checking the country of origin, alcohol content and other relevant information about it, as I come across a printed document on the other side of the large stack, previously out of sight from our view. It's a delivery order. It details these very same pallets being delivered here, to this address. According to the document the delivery was made only a few weeks ago, but that's not what surprises me. It's the name on the receiving person's field on the form. I quickly stick the delivery order back to the plastic wrapper covering the massive tower, take my liberated bottle of booze and we start moving back through the long building to exit the barn.

Once we get out of the building, the sun starts to leave progressively longer streaks of light across the surrounding fields. It's finally getting dark.

"Ey, this not bad. I would even pay money for it. Not much, but hey, booze is booze" Alex says as he takes few more sips from his bottle. It is some sort of 20% ABV vodka based flavoured drink, presumably ideal for parties like this, where it's mixed into a cocktail. We, however don't bother with mixing. It goes well on its own.

"Ready to go boys?" Sonya asks as she sees us approach from the distance, each holding a bottle. "You two are really resourceful. Did you already run to the store from here? Thirst really knows no limits."

"Is from my own personal secret stash" Alex says with a sly tone. "Would you ladies like a try of my latest find? I see Filip is still best friends with his own bottle." He points at the slightly drunk guy sitting next to the car, humming along to the music playing inside.

M brings some cups from the car, Alex pours out some of the drink and we take one last quick look around the party grounds. Me, Alex, Filip and Sonya drinking from plastic cups and carrying them around this place feels like we were either very late or very early to another round of the party. To think that this field used to be completely built up with stages, booths and makeshift paths makes me appreciate the speed at which nature reclaims its territory once people leave. I visualise the opposite facing stages where artists used to battle each other with how loud each could play. I remember the massive decorations set up across the trees, tens of metres wide. But now just a setting sun and singing birds fill the site.

"Me and M talked it over and we have decided to drop you off at the port to Volkonsk. From there you're on your own, though" Sonya says. "We've come this far and it would feel wrong to cut the party short now."

"I won't argue with that" I confirm with a happy tone. "You're welcome to join us on the island if you change your mind though. Plenty more time for party there."

"We should really get going if we want to catch the last ferry" M says, as she grows bored being the only sober person there. "If we start now, we should arrive just in time." The port is an hour and a half drive from Bardok, followed by a half hour ferry ride and then another half hour to get to the campsite. We never went there to tent though, we always rented the small huts right next to the beach, made a fire in the sand and cooked our food right there. It's the ultimate getaway - sea, silence and yes, finally, pines and junipers. I don't ever plan to go back to the city.

The air is cool, but still plenty more warm than any day this year so far. We pack ourselves back in the car and an overall calm washes over me. Maybe it's because it's getting late, maybe it has just been a long day. We start driving nevertheless. M starts the car, shifts into gear and we are off. On the road, again.

Part 5 - 2105

BOOM. The car stops. We had just gone a hundred metres from the kolkhoz and suddenly we come to a complete halt. Everyone is thrown up from their seats and then slam back down. The sound is exactly like a bomb exploded right in front of us. Everyone in the car falls silent.

"Well, that's not good" I say after a small pause. "I'm drinking, who's with me?" Alex eagerly raises his hand.

"Is probably just a blown tire," Filip says, trying to look out of the window. "Have little more faith in my car. Is built to be bomb proof."

"Well it's not a blown petrol tank, that's for sure. Otherwise we would be sitting in the field there" I reply and point to the massive empty plot of land next to us. "Also, it's still not your car" I yell at him.

"I will agree with Filip on this one, Vova built it up to withstand more pounding than it originally ever could" Sonya says.

We all step out of the car, but find no visible damage to it. All tires intact, no smoke rising. However, a large pothole lay behind the car that M must have hit as she was driving in pitch black darkness. We must have missed it on our drive in.

"Well *there's* your problem" I say as I'm pondering how this happened. "That thing is big enough to swallow an elephant. But still doesn't explain the car stopping. Give it another go, M."

She tries to start the car, but nothing happens. No clicking, no engine turning, just silence and the jingling of the keychain attached to the car's single key.

"Shit, I've run through holes bigger than that. I crashed into wall few times with it and it ran perfect" Filip boasts.

"That's some quality sales tactic there, debil. Sonya just bought it from you today. Now she knows it's a piece of junk because of you" Alex exclaims.

"What? I'm just saying it can endure worse. Besides, what she going to do, give it back?" Filip says.

"Okay, guys, there's no buyer's remorse here," Sonya says to stop them from bickering. "I'm very happy with the purchase, especially for the price. I'm sure there's a logical reason for all of this."

I open the hood to inspect any possible damage to the engine. "What the holy fucking shit is this?" I yell across the fields, scaring away the wildlife in a ten kilometre radius. "I've seen better order in a pig farm."

Everyone gathers around the front of the car. The sight that greets us is absolutely comedical and simultaneously maddening.

"Filip, did you try repair this after drinking five litres of vodka or what?" I ask the former owner. "Look at this massive bundle of wires coming from the battery. What is half this shit for? Where do these all even lead?" I observe the engine bay and try to look for a logical explanation for the bootleg repairs.

Filip, looking more smug than ever, has a reasonable answer for once. "Hah! Joke's on you. I never even opened the hood once! That shit had to be there before me. Probably that kid that sold it to me tried to do some gopnik repairs and add underglow or something."

"I actually know what that might be," Sonya stopped us once again. "Vova used to have tons of extra gear on this car. Electronics, lights, engine management, you know the tech they used for racing. He probably had to remove that stuff to make it street legal to sell, but didn't really bother making it drivable for very long."

"An ECU on a fucking Lada? This guy truly had to be crazy" I reply. "But say what you want, the car ran smooth as silk for longer than some '05s even live. Having said that, I'm not repairing that. Not in the dark with no tools. Most likely the electronics system shorted itself out once we hit that pothole. We could play connect the dots here for hours, trying to unfuck this mess, but we have more chance of a lightning strike" I say as I poke the massive bundle of wires, still looking for a logical cause of the problem. "Alex, didn't your work friend use to live near here? Maybe he could pick us up?"

"Vassili the vandal? He moved to the capital city. Big man with big import-export business now," Alex replies.

I slam closed the hood, grab a bottle from Alex, take a big hit and sit on the ground. The faint aroma of pines and junipers gradually starts to fade from my imagination.

"We could still call roadside help. It's expensive, but at least we can get going" Sonya suggests.

"No point, they will just tow us back to Garvostok. And I don't know about you but I'm not turning back until I get to that fucking island. You can go, I'm hitchhiking to Volkonsk if I need to."

"I'm with Lev," Alex starts. "I'm not going back. The only way is forward. We got this far, I won't let some faulty car electronics stop me now. I say let's wait for the morning and put our heads together and fix this mess in the daylight. Now we just have to wait till morning for sunrise. Which is just five short hours away. Not a problem."

"Sounds good to me" I reply. "Sonya, I saw some orange blankets in the trunk there. They there for the taking?"

"Oh, I completely forgot about those. Sure, they're some comforters I got from a promotion" Sonya says and pops open the trunk. Wa each take one of the large orange blankets with a booze brand logo on the front.

"Blin, if this not keep us warm, I'm not sure what will" I say jokingly, looking at Alex and pointing to the brand printed on the blankets.

"I call back seat. You can feed the mosquitos here if you want" Filip replies and jumps in the car, cuddles up to his bottle and goes to sleep.

"He's probably slept back there more than in his own bed. Come, Lev, let's move the car more out of way so nobody crashes into it in the meantime. It's in middle of the road" Alex suggests.

"Crash into it? Really? It's a dead end street that ends with an abandoned kolkhoz. Who's gonna drive here? The ghost of Soviet past? Or maybe a KGB operative on a bicycle? We're probably the only people who have been here for over a year. I bet you a case of beer nobody will drive past here. You could spend your night sleeping on the road and you'd be safe."

"No bet. Also, you can take the gravel road if you want, I'm setting up on the grass" Alex says and points at a small clearing near our stopped car.

We proceed to place our blankets on the grass and lay down. Me and Sonya near the car, Alex and M further away, as they have started chatting quite a bit after arriving at Bardok and seem very secretive with their private conversation.

I place my bag under my head and enjoy the serene environment. The night is quiet, almost silent. Only the sound of a few birds can be heard, mixed with the laughter of Alex in the distance. A clear starry sky reveals itself from what little clouds there were earlier and the air is filled with the smell of fresh grass.

"No mosquitos" I say with relief. "It's lucky, because I'm usually the biggest mosquito magnet out of everyone. I would wake up covered in hundreds of bites. Still worth it though. I wonder if it's the parties that scared them away those years ago and they never simply returned."

Sonya laughs and replies. "It's just the nature here. There's no bodies of water nearby, so the only flying objects are the birds. What little insects there are, are dinner for them."

"You know a lot about the area. You from around here?"

"I think you already know," she calmly replies.

"I think I already know."

"I think you want to ask me something" she says, laying on her blanket, having turned to face my direction.

I pause. "Yes. I wonder how many leaves of grass did I crush by setting this blanket down. This thing is massive!"

She starts laughing and replies "that's definitely one of the many philosophical questions in life. I mean the other thing."

A longer pause. Then a deep sigh. Then I present my question. "You own this place, don't you?"

She lays back and takes a sigh of relief. "I inherited it when I turned 18. I'm not exactly sure how my grandparents acquired it, but they left it all to me. They probably thought it was a great chance for me to make something with my life. Farming isn't really my thing as you can see."

"Really? I can really imagine you wielding a pitchfork and herding pigs. You seem very much at home here."

"No, not really. But I didn't have the heart to sell this place either. This enchanting ruin that time has long forgotten."

"So, is that why you let people use this place for the parties?"

She pauses for a while. "For two years after getting this land, nothing much happened. I came to check on it a few times, but that was it. Then I got in touch with some people and it basically snowballed from there."

"Sounds fine as long as you don't mind thousands of people trampling over your precious land."

"There's not much to trample. Look at this place, the state of it is bad as it is. They couldn't possibly make it worse. Besides, I like having people around. It makes this place feel alive."

"Sorry about liberating the drinks, by the way. I will find a way to repay you somehow."

"Yeah I assumed that's where you got them. Especially considering I'm the only one importing that brand to the country. You could repay me with something warm for cover, if you have anything in your bag. It's getting very chilly." The wind picks up and once again reminds me it's spring.

"Nothing like that here, sorry" I say as I browse through my work bag. "Just work stuff. You can cover yourself with your blanket though and use mine to lay down. Besides, being closer is very beneficial. Thermodynamically speaking. Especially considering our unexpected sleeping arrangement in the wilderness."

"I wouldn't call my farm the wilderness," she says with a laugh. "But I see your point. Very diplomatic."

"Well, the other option is the pig barn where you stashed your tower of drinks, but to be honest, I couldn't take the smell for another minute, let alone for a whole night." She agrees and comes over to my blanket as I make room for her on mine.

"Must be a headache mowing the grass of 20 hectares though," I tell her as she settles down beside me while I look at the starry sky. She snuggles tight into her blanket, covering herself completely. Just a nose, eyes and flowing light brown hair peek out from under it. She looks like she's completely freezing. I feel slight guilt as I feel the need to remove my shoes and roll up the sleeves on my jacket to cool down. I'm simply built for cold weather.

"Actually it's 40" say the small nose and peeking eyes that appear from under the orange blanket. She removes the comforter from over her mouth to speak more clearly. "There's 20 hectares around the kolkhoz area and 20 more next to it. That's where we are now."

I am surprised at her modest tone when she speaks about owning such a massive plot of land. "Seriously? That's the size of a small town. Think of all the possibilities. I would be happy with a 10 by 10 metre plot of land in the middle of forest. One small sauna, one grill for shashlik. I don't need much."

"It's odd. This land came so easily for me and I've never thought of it as being more than an inconvenience. And then there's others dreaming of owning just a fraction of something similar. But in reality it's actually a fact that..." she pauses. "I feel embarrassed even saying it to you directly, but you've been a big inspiration for me."

I look toward her in the moonlit night to try and read her expression more clearly. "Me?" I ask her inquisitively. "What do you mean? I sing to mildly intoxicated people at rock concerts. Hardly what I'd call a pillar of modern society."

"You're being modest. You've built yourself up from nothing and have come so far. You're the reason I even started these events" she says slowly. "My biggest regret is that I never got you to play at them."

A single cold chill runs down my spine and my face drops. I suddenly realise what she's talking about. I quickly sit up, look at her still wrapped in the massive blanket. "Wait." I stand up. "Hold on." I take a step back. "What?"

"The events sort of naturally pivoted toward EDM music, the final lineup never would've made sense with a rock band.

I'm sorry. First I planned a small event to invite local artists, but..." she says, sitting up.

"Hold on" I say and take another step back. "You said what?" I am now standing next to the car. "You *did* what?"

"Are you alright?" she asks.

"Uh, no. You're talking about the Bardok parties? Ten thousand attendants and tens of top artists from around the world? *You* created that? You have legendary status among us. We talk about you as if some divine miracle that makes parties appear out of thin air." I tell her with some visible craziness in my eyes.

"It's a bit more complex than that. It's really a long story" she starts. "Actually, it's not that long. I sort of invited all my..."

I interrupt her explanation. "Hold on, the Bardok parties were arranged by SonicBarracuda, everyone knows that. That's some agency that promoted the thing for months each year. Organised the stages, the artists, the vendors..."

She stands up and reaches her hand out for a shake. "SonicBarracuda, nice to meet you." This slim young woman standing in front of me shocks me with the biggest piece of information I have received in years. "It was just my dumb username and it sort of stuck. I'd tell you not to tell anyone about my secret, but nobody would probably believe you anyway."

I stand next to the car, frozen. Taking my precious time to arrange my thoughts into coherent words before I allow my mouth to make a sound. "Nooo... You can't be. I don't believe it." I tell her abruptly. Without hesitation she reaches into her pocket, takes her phone and opens social media apps one after another revealing being logged in to the account responsible for organising and promoting the whole event - SonicBarracuda. It's unquestionably her. My eyes get progressively bigger. "No, no, no. No! I've been hanging around with the Bardok organiser this whole day? I don't believe it!" I say dismissively and start walking away into the pitch black darkness toward the city.

"Are you alright? Please don't leave. I really don't like the dark here" she says as she starts slowly running toward me, holding the neon orange comforter around her and pointing her phone's flashlight in my direction, it bouncing as she runs. "Please?" she says desperately.

I stop walking toward the endless pitch black darkness. "*You...*" I start saying hesitantly. "*You're* the most famous event organiser... in the *country*? And nobody knows who you are?"

"Well, we all have our secrets," she says quietly.

The few scattered clouds in the sky start to pour out small drops of the same familiar cold rain that welcomed me after the evening's bus ride. "But you're one person. That's fucking extraordinary. How did you ever manage it all?" I ask Sonya, who's now standing in front of me, getting soaked by the increasingly heavier rain.

"Well, I was highly motivated. I did it for you. I mean the artists. I mean…" She suddenly stops talking, apparently having embarrassed herself. "I mean, it was meant to be a small event, but it sort of snowballed."

"It snowballed… into the biggest rave in the whole country? That's fucking crazy. So how do I fit into this? Did you just expect me to walk by one day and you'd introduce yourself as the event planner and invite me or something?"

"Actually I didn't think it through that far. I just wanted to hang out and talk or whatever. You've been an inspiration for me for years. Just wanted to give my thanks. I started inviting all sorts of artists. I assumed you would be on the list to appear, being locally based. In the end so many EDM ones signed up and people really liked the lineup and…"

"But wait, I never even got an invite to play. I wasn't really expecting one either, though. You know, most normal people just come up to talk if they want to start a conversation."

"At your concert? Lev, please. I was a random girl in the crowd. You wouldn't probably have seen me as more than another fan."

"You're not wrong there. I will admit, this is a significantly more impressive approach than a fan mail letter or an invite to tea."

Quickly the rain gets worse, now becoming more than a slight inconvenience.

"I think that pig barn is starting to sound more and more attractive" I tell Sonya, who's blanket is quickly getting more moist by the second.

She raises her voice to speak over the increasing rain. "Come on!" Sonya starts running toward the kolkhoz houses. I pick up my blanket and work bag and follow her, lighting my path with my phone's flashlight. We arrive at what looks like a small family house next to the kolkhoz courtyard. She reaches under the small flower pot on the windowsill next to the main door, picks up a key and proceeds to open the door to the house.

"You *are* full of surprises," I tell her. I look around the inside of the small house. "Well, it's significantly better than the pig barn. Oh shit, I need to go check on Alex and M," I suddenly remember.

"Don't worry about them. They went to the woodcutting shed. M told me they'll go there once we sat down on the blankets. It's not as cosy as this place, but much better than the open sky in this weather. Come on, you can take the big bed."

She shows me around the small house, guiding me toward what looks like the master bedroom. I kick off my shoes and without hesitation fall on the bed, dead tired.

"I guess tea is out of the question then?" she asks hesitantly, standing in the doorway.

"You know what, I think under these circumstances, tea sounds great." I say as I pull myself up from the bed. "So M knew all along. They didn't just accidentally find the toolshed in the woods right?"

"Woodcutting shed, yes. She's one of the few people who knows about all of this. Given how cautious she is, I'm guessing your friend Alex still doesn't know. He probably thinks they're lucky to have gotten away from the rain just in time."

"Yes, I doubt us and our sleeping arrangement is what's on his mind right now. He probably forgot who he even came here with. I, however, have many questions for you."

Me and Sonya walk to the kitchen, the sound of rain still coming from the outside. None of the lights in the house are working, presumably due to the electricity being switched off. She finds some candles, lights them and proceeds to light the gas stove as well, then places a large metal kettle on the stove.

"I probably have more questions than you. But you go first. Otherwise we'll both fall asleep before I get to finish," she says as she sits down at the small kitchen table. The table is covered with a white lace tablecloth, straight from the 1970s. The two small candles emit a warm light across the whole room.

"I guess the main question is, what was your plan if the car didn't break down?"

"Oh, straight to the point. No philosophical inquiries about how many leaves of grass we crushed running over here?"

"I was planning to leave the important questions for later. But seriously, you offered to take us to the port to Volkonsk today. You would have dropped us off and never probably seen us again."

"I didn't really think that far. I guess I'm just lucky the car broke down."

We proceed to talk about our careers and achievements for another hour, drinking the chamomile tea she made. The sun starts to show its warm glow over the horizon, peeking beyond the forest. The rain has stopped and left behind a strong smell of wet grass. Sonya, starting to show first signs of tiredness, goes to check the back room for her sleeping arrangements. I take this time to quickly get to my bed and rest my eyes. I drop down on the bed like a log, making the pillows on the spring mattress bounce up and a small cloud of dust to blow from below the bed. I close my eyes for a second, imagining still of the endless forests of pine, like a dehydrated wanderer in the desert, longing for a single drop of water.

Part 6 - Market

I startle myself up. How long is she going to be, looking at the second bedroom? I start getting up from the bed, but quickly get hit in the eyes with a gleaming bright light. My eyes are burning as I try to rub them, letting my brain get accustomed to the situation. I sit up on the bed as I attempt to understand what's going on. There's a bright light coming from the kitchen. There's a bright light coming from the bedroom window. I finally clear my eyes. Oh shit, it's morning. I just dropped down on the bed literally a second ago. I don't even remember dreaming. I stand up.

"WHOA!" I yell as I am startled by what appears in front of me. A person sleeping in the armchair next to the bed, covered by an orange comforter. I slowly start to understand what's going on.

"Lev, you startled me," the sleepy orange bundle says on the armchair. It reveals itself to be Sonya.

"My god, you fucking shocked me. What are you doing here? Wait, how is it morning already? How long was I out? Didn't you go to the other bedroom?" All the questions come out as one continuous line of speech.

"Other bedroom? This is the only one in the house. I think you fell asleep around 2," she says sleepily.

Okay that was strange. "Were you planning on sleeping in the armchair all along?" I ask her.

"Umm… I didn't think that far ahead," she says with slight embarrassment.

"Alright I'm beginning to see a pattern here." Event organising mastermind with no skill of planning her own life more than two seconds ahead. I take out my phone to check the time. The battery is dead. Shit. I must have forgotten the flashlight on all night. "Please tell me you have a charger in the car."

"Sorry, I haven't gotten around to putting one in yet. You can check the time on my phone on the kitchen table, though."

The details of the inside of the house slowly start to register with my eyes as I begin my walk toward the kitchen. The walls covered in colourful wallpaper, the coloured floorboards squeaking with every step. The morning sun shining in from the white lace curtains leaves a distinct pattern on the kitchen cupboards. I pick up the phone covered with a flower-printed case and check the time. It's two hours past noon. "I was going to say good morning, but I'm afraid we missed that opportunity." I open the kitchen window. "Well hello people of the forest! How was the tool shed motel?" Alex and M are sitting on wooden lawn chairs on the porch behind the house.

"What fucking miracle woke you up?" Alex says, holding a half smoked cigarette in his mouth. "Come get some coffee, wake you up good."

I look at the pot of coffee and biscuits on the porch table. "When the blin did you make this?"

"The biscuits are provided by our good friend global economy, but the coffee M made like an hour ago. I'm not even surprised you didn't hear us. You look like you had a wild night, we've been walking and talking for hours. Did you know Sonya owns this house?"

"No, I just assumed she broke in like normal people," I tell Alex sarcastically. I go outside into the warm weather. It feels even hotter today. I reach for my sunglasses from my bag and put them on. The sun instantly warms me up and feels hot on my skin. I proceed to sit down on the chair by the porch table and pour myself a cup of coffee. "What century are these biscuits from?"

"Not sure. Haven't killed me yet." Alex takes one more and a sip of coffee with it.

Sonya joins us outside, still looking sleepy, presumably from having the least comfortable sleeping arrangement of us all. We all drink some more coffee, but shortly decide it's time to get going. Me and Alex take our cups and walk to the car, where our repairs are set to begin on the allegedly notoriously reliable racing car. Alex rips open the back door, screams Filip's name and slams the door closed. Filip jumps up, still holding on to his half bottle of brandy, visibly confused about the daylight.

"You assholes. I was having beautiful dream. I was farmer, milking cows."

"Oh good, you're up farmer man," I tell the freshly awoken passenger. "No time for decoding your unconscious hallucinations. Go to the small house and ask them for all the tools they can find. I don't care if it's bottle opener or hammer. We need to fix this cyka just enough to get it started once. Let's just hope the fucking alternator didn't end itself."

The afternoon sun beats down on us as we attempt to fix the mystery issue with the Lada. The problem with these old Soviet cars is that every issue they have is a mystery. You could be a master mechanic, work on these cars for decades and still a new unique problem would arise, demanding a completely new approach to fix. Presumably that's why every owner knew how to work on them. Needless to say, the custom upgrades that were made on the car didn't help our case. The visibly aftermarket parts were easily recognisable and dismissable from the list of faults. It's the mix of old and new parts that was most likely causing the issue. Alex, Filip and I work on the problem for an hour. Alex mostly suggesting solutions he would find online and Filip repeating how his other cars never had this issue. I disconnect the battery and try to make sense of the melon-sized bundle of wires that spider out into the car's chassis. Multiple wires lead to plugs that seem to do absolutely nothing. Some connectors broken, some filled with dirt and dust over time, some ends simply have stripped wiring. Filip is sitting in the driver seat, turning the key from time to time checking for signs of life, as I attempt to remove more and more wires with dead ends.

"How does this even happen? These things are unkillable. You know it could be some completely new problem," I tell Alex, who's standing next to me, as idealess as me.

"Sometimes the simplest solution is the best one." Alex takes a big wrench and hits the engine multiple times with force, leaving a few dents in the carburetor. I'm leaning over the engine bay, watching this amazing work of precision. He then kicks the bumper and throws the wrench on the ground. "Give it a go, Filip." The engine starts. Me and Alex look at each other, pause for a moment and shake hands.

"Very well done, doctor. Great work." Me and Alex sit in the back, Filip turns the car around and drives it to the kolkhoz courtyard, ending in a long powerslide on the loose gravel. I roll down the window. "Next stop, port to Volkonsk."

We pack our things and the orange blankets. I grab my bag and sit in the back. Sonya and M quickly tidy the outside, lock the house and jump in the car. Who knows how long this car will run. We're just happy to get going. Filip takes on the role of driver and we start our journey toward the port. On the way we refuel the car at the petrol station, leaving it to run just in case it decides not to start again. The drive goes smooth and quick, no further interruptions from the engine. After an hour and a half of driving, we arrive at the port. We say our goodbyes, the car still running on hopes and dreams. Sonya and M start their drive back to the capital city. We buy the ferry tickets and get on the half hour long ride to the island. I'm starting to feel the success of arrival.

"So, Lev. Good night?" Alex confronts me as we lean on the railings of the ferry, looking as the waves flow by.

"Good? That was the strangest night I've had in years. I don't know what she put in that tea, but I was knocked out cold."

"Your loss, the woodcutting shed was very eventful. You at least get number of that Sonya girl?"

"Actually, I didn't think that far ahead." A strange familiarity comes from saying it.

"Your loss, M said she'll be joining us on the island later this week."

The ferry arrives on the island and we disembark along with the many cars. The weather is windy and the smell of seaweed pushes its way to my nose. I rub my hands together. "So, who do we know in Volkonsk? Alex, you still got the number of that woman from the community centre?"

"Oksana? I'm pretty sure her husband is the mayor now. I doubt she'll want to be seen with us again. But you never know, let's see how the week goes," he says mysteriously. Alex snaps his fingers. "I have an idea." He takes his phone, takes a picture of the ferry in the port and posts it. "Check this out. Wait and watch," he says. Less than ten minutes later, a car approaches with music playing as loud as the inside of a club. A red 90s station wagon with steel wheels pulls up right in front of us.

"Friends! You finally decided to leave city behind," says the person jumping out of the car. It's Vitali. "You come exactly at right time. We have big event tomorrow. Whole island will be attending the county fair."

"Tomorrow? That leaves us only one day to catch up and liberate some vodka from its bottle-shaped prison," I tell him. "Vitali, let's hit the market. I have some ideas."

"Ooooy, I better warn the salesmen," Vitali replies with excitement. "Every time you hit the market, the whole island economy goes into chaos. What is it this time? Kebab? Cabbage rolls?"

"I work with what I have. We all getting fed."

"Lev, you playing for us today? I know at least half the crowd want to see your concert," Vitali says.

"With what? Pots and pans? All I brought is work laptop. I can probably mix together nature sounds and scream over that."

"Nooo no no. You haven't heard? There's new local band. My brother plays drums there. They'll be performing at the fair. I'm sure I can talk him into playing few of your tracks with you too. I wouldn't be surprised if he's got all the gear to produce your sound."

Alex and Filip, who have just lit their second cigarette since getting off the ferry, look at each other, then back at me. "Blin, not problem," Alex replies. "Give me set list and a bass and I give a world-class concert." Alex does a quick riff on air guitar. "Filip can do security."

"Security at *your* concert? Last time your crowd nearly burned the stage down," Filip replies. "This small place though, I can handle."

"Then it's settled!" Vitali exclaims. "Give me a short set list and my brother will be ready for you at fair. I'll get the organiser to squeeze you in to the main stage, no problem." We sit in the car and start driving to the market in town centre, planning the event along the way.

For a small town the crowd is always surprisingly active. We must have not been the only ones who realised that warm weather should be utilised to the maximum. I spot a phone charger in Vitali's car. I plug it in and start up my phone. The data connection synchronises my notifications. Thirteen work emails and just one from the manager asking if I'm working from home, since he didn't see me in the office. I consider replying, but since the workday has already ended, I disregard the obligations and turn the phone back off. I disconnect the charger.

"Trouble in corporate life? Bossman not happy with your abrupt disappearance?" Alex asks.

"Trouble? It has to be a very fragile organisation if my single day disappearance makes the whole corporation crumble. They will manage. I probably call tomorrow, say I'm working remotely, not to be disturbed until next week. They never ask, I never tell. Half my work is automated anyway, other half not time sensitive. Let's party."

Alex claps his hands together in excitement. "Hit it, Vitali! We hungry."

Vitali drives us to the town market and parks his car by the entrance. We are greeted with a wide variety of smells and sounds coming from the seemingly endless rows of stalls, stands and vendors. People walking around, everyone with a purpose or a place to get to. Some browsing the market, some walking right through. The view of this open-air market stuns me as I have never seen this place so alive. This is already the third time I've been here and yet never seen it this busy. The market is a mix of modern technology and Soviet engineering. Some vendors using ancient looking scales, others digital screens and card terminals. There's a constant noise of overlapping voices and small stereos playing music. The babushkas selling their fresh potato watching over their produce like hawks. The vibrant colours shine from the stalls as a fresh bed of wild flowers on a field on the first day of summer. Many stalls are packed with a variety of smoked sausages, luring people in with free samples. One salesman without a stand is selling his smoked meats right off the back of his bicycle. I start looking for the best looking cucumbers around, but all the offerings are equally appealing and fresh. The bright green colour of the clean washed produce glistening in the sun is only comparable to memories of such visions from childhood. "Ten kilograms of cucumber" I tell the stall vendor I have picked out from the rest. Dill, blackcurrant leaves and garlic I get from the other stalls nearby. On the far end of the market is a large house with simply the sign "meat" hanging high above it. It's a refrigerated place with vendors here only selling different fresh meats. I enter the cold house and get hit in the face with a strong smell of fish. Proud fishermen standing behind their stalls with their daily catch. Some sitting quietly, others calling buyers near with promises of theirs being the freshest product. Butchers with large heaps of pork, beef and many varieties of products made from the meat fill most of the building. Minced, marinated, fresh, some even selling half-prepared products like cutlets and sausages. Everything is looking ready to be thrown on a fire and cooked to perfection right this minute. But I am not looking for half-made stuff. I pick the vendor with the largest heap of pork and order him to wrap me up 20 kilograms of the finest stuff he has. He jokingly asks if I wouldn't want to buy the whole pig instead, but I decline his offer with a promise to come back for more later. I carry the several heavy bags back to the car.

"Are we feeding a whole army? Lev, how long you planning on being here?" Alex quickly asks as I approach the car.

"I have plan, Alex."

"That you always do. But a ton of cucumber and pork? Are we starting a restaurant?" He quickly realises. "YOU'RE DOING THE FOOD TRUCK!" Alex yells and cheers.

"Quiet down, the whole town will hear of my bootleg operation." I soon hear my name being called out from the crowd. I look at Alex. "You see what you have done." I quickly recognise the person calling me, now running toward me with enthusiasm. It's Oscar. He shakes my hand and catches his breath.

"You're back. And you starting the food truck? Let me help. I have my sources for the best ingredients," he says.

I met Oscar the last time I was in Volkonsk, around a table of drinks. He wore then and is today again wearing a white apron, as if always working at the market. His enthusiasm about food is only surpassed by his enthusiasm to cook more of it. The market is undoubtedly the most likely place to find him.

"Good to see you too, but can you keep it the hell down? They going to put me in jail for running an illegal operation here" I tell the very enthusiastic Oscar. Not sure if it's the sun that made everyone seemingly over-crazy but here we are.

"You need the licence? Hah! Getting that is easier than a hit in the head. I've helped tons of people get them. I'll get one for you by tomorrow, no problem. People won't even have to know you have it, you keep your bootleg image and we both swim in money. One condition though, you only use my produce."

"And what, you charge me arm and leg for each cucumber and tomato I buy from you?"

"Hah! Compared to these market prices, I'm giving these away to you. You would not believe how much they cash in on the markets. Yes I'm looking at you, farmer Fedya," he yells at a vendor, who's looking at him. "Yeah I know where you grow your potatoes. So what you think, Lev? Let's do some business, make some money? I still remember the queue behind your food stall last time."

"I say why not. Let's feed some people. Any idea where to get an actual food truck though?" I ask him.

"I have friend, he has something even better. Not even need truck. Trailer, cleared out and a portable kitchen slammed inside. Gas stove and everything. No petrol tank to go boom. No coal grill to burn down. Hitch it behind car and good to go. Only thing is, it's an old horse trailer he rebuilt as a food van. I'm sure the smell of horse is all but gone."

"What is it with the fucking farm animals on this trip?" I ask Alex.

"Speaking of animals," Alex starts speaking with clear enthusiasm. "Back in Bardok in the woodshed..."

I quickly stop him and turn back to Oscar. "Let's do it. Have it ready tomorrow with the licence, bring it by Vitali's house. By the way, you selling onions today?"

Oscar turns around, runs to his stall, picks a whole bag of onions and hands them over. "Here, on the house. Oy, this going to be good," he says with excitement.

We set off, stopping by the store for some more ingredients and condiments the market could not provide. I feel the excitement start to get into me. No more lazy days in the smog-filled capital city.

Volkonsk is a sparsely populated island mainly filled with locals, but often visited by tourists, either from abroad or from within the country. The two thousand people living here locally have a tendency to attend nearly every event on the 200 square kilometre island. This often leads to anything happening around here, including the town market, to feel like a massive festival.

"Vitali, you still living at the edge of the world? I need to use your kitchen and some industrial equipment." This is not the first time I have asked him that, so he already looks visibly excited about it. He agrees, on one condition, that I join them for the bonfire later that night. We arrive at Vitali's small country house. For someone who lives alone on the far edge of an island with less people than an average New York apartment building, he has a very well kept garden and lawn. I don't bother with admiring the scenery for too long. I have a mission. I know what I need to do. Alex, Vitali and Filip take it on themselves to start building a bonfire, downing a case of beer and talking important business while doing so. I find all the closable containers in the house - jars, bowls, pots and lidded food containers. The conveyor belt level of efficiency of preparation that starts in the kitchen would be enough to impress a global audience. A short hour later, I emerge from the kitchen and walk outside to where the guys are still collecting material for what now is a house-height stack of wood.

"I hope you don't mind I had to clear out your refrigerator, Vitali."

"As long as you kept the freezer intact and full of vodka, is all good. You know you smell like a slaughterhouse right?"

"Yes. The smell of money," I reply.

Alex approaches me with concern. "You did all that for tomorrow. What about today? We eat berries from the bushes in Vitali's garden and drink rainwater?"

"I have an idea. Vitali, you don't mind some company, no?" I go inside, find a phone charger and wait for my mobile device to power up. I type up the coordinates of our location with a note that simply says "bring sausages and beer" and post it publicly on my social media. Likes and comments start to flow in immediately. Some asking for explanation, some confirming that they're on their way. I interact with none of it. My job here is done. I leave the device to recharge and join the other comrades outside. I take one of the cold beers and sit down as we light the massive bonfire from four sides. We talk for fifteen minutes, remembering the good times and hoping the best are yet to come. Soon someone approaches in a car, steps into the yard, quickly observes the lawn and house.

"This the place?" the stranger asks.

I look at him holding a small case of beer. "This is the place." We watch this complete stranger come up, sit down and we start talking as if we were long time friends. Merely five more minutes pass and a group of three people approaches from the same direction. I wave them in, confirming they have arrived at the right place.

"Lev, what did you do?" Vitali asks, not with fear in his voice, but a sincere tone of curiosity.

"I did what I could. Enjoy the sausages." I take the free food the strangers brought to the bonfire and greet them as they were the people I was expecting all along. In no time tens of people appear, then a hundred total. We quickly go from having no food to being the most well stocked house on the island. Almost everyone brought something for the event. A massive turnout for a random Tuesday, especially on Volkonsk. Some of the guests brought speakers and start blasting music from them. One brought a guitar, expecting a live performance. I do not let them down. The gathering looks from the side as if an organised party is taking place, but it is simply a bonfire with good company. Some people arrive from the mainland, some from island. I tell everyone to find me at the fair tomorrow with the food truck and bring two friends. I start to get a feeling I didn't buy enough meat. The pines and junipers are near, but still so far. I must find them the next day. Not much further now.

Part 7 - County fair

I wake up with the worst fucking feeling ever. It's not a headache. It's not a hangover. It's the feeling of regret. Regret that I can't do this every day. I take a look around and try to remember how I got to sleep. I sit up on my bed and soon realise it is a couch that I have woken up on. Looking around the room I realise that the low sun shining in from the windows indicates a very early morning hour. It's going to be another sunny day. I equip my sunglasses and start working my way to the outside. I stop at the kitchen dinner table as I spot a small pile of what looks like handwritten notes. This wasn't here yesterday. I take one and squint my eyes to understand anything from the scribble. It is undoubtedly a fan mail letter, addressed to me. Probably can't really call it "mail" since it was hand delivered. I slowly move my body outside and start getting memory flashbacks of what happened last night and how. The sounds, the people, the fire. The unmistakable smell of a bonfire coming off my jacket indicates my proximity to the actual flame last night. I remember a girl. She was very friendly. Maybe too friendly. I quickly check my pockets for my personal belongings, then my bag. It's common practice for me every time at a larger gathering. All the things still appear in order and in their place, other than a note in my bag that I decide to investigate later. I step outside into the morning sun. The heat from it slowly warms my face and I check the time on my phone. It's six in the morning. Shit. Why am I awake? I check my gallery for recent images and a long series of pictures reveal themselves of last night, ending at around four in the morning. Two hours of sleep is better than no hours of sleep. I walk around the garden and bonfire. Stacks of empty boxes and heaps of empty beer cans decorate the lawn. Too tired to deal with this now. The lawn chairs around the fireplace remind me of a guitar I had in my hand yesterday. I signed it and then played it. And then... burned it? No. It is now too valuable to destroy. I lay down on a lawn recliner and try remember more of the night.

"You were out here all night?" Alex asks.

I look at him, surprised at where he appeared from. "What are you son of forest? Where you come from?" I quickly deduce from my clear head and the much brighter sun that I had fallen asleep. I check my phone and see it's noon. "Shit, I did it again."

"Did what? Fell asleep next to the girl instead of on top of her again?" Alex says with a laugh. "Oh wait in your case, in the next bed from the girl," he laughs some more, lights a cigarette and sits on the next lawn recliner.

"You ass, you know exactly my situation." I signal him to pass me the cigarette. I take a drag and pass it back. "Mmm... Like exercising in a cement factory."

"Hey you the one who wanted be famous band singer. Would you be regular normal person like me, nobody care who you do or don't do and you need to work for their attention like everyone else. Wake up next to one woman or three. Is your life."

"That your way of saying that what happened to you last night?"

He takes a long drag and looks at me in confusion. "You really don't remember shit from last night, huh? Maybe a beer to freshen your mind?"

"Actually not a bad idea, I feel fucking great." I look around the area for a full container of alcohol. Most beer cases reveal themselves to be empty but after a short search I find one live one. I grab a can, pop open the drink and ask Alex to tell me the story of the previous night. As he goes through last night's events, I quickly remember every moment of it.

"You at least remember the girl, right?" Alex asks.

"I remember the girl. Very friendly one right?"

"Friendly is putting it mildly, she was a true dedicated fan. She seemed genuinely happy to have gotten so close to the infamous Lev."

"Shit, that's right. Was she smoking last night? I still have the taste of ash in my mouth."

"I maybe gave her one or two. You know, for someone so concerned about repercussions, you really have a hard time saying no to people."

"Why say no? Is very rude. They always have such good things to say. That's like doing a concert and asking the people to not clap and cheer."

"You and your band metaphors. You know, normal people stopped looking for clowns in the circus, once they found them in the mirror."

"That's some solid life advice. We should call the food truck that. Clown In Your Mirror."

"No, that sounds like a low budget horror movie. Plus, people will be expecting a clown in the truck and I doubt Filip wants to take on the role. I was thinking more along the lines of 'Pleased to Meat You,' but now saying it out loud, that sounds like a backyard adult film. Or a high-end Hollywood movie about an animated talking pig that goes to work in the hospitality industry."

I take a sip of the beer in my hand. "I would watch that movie. The pig would be called Fred. Fred the friendly concierge. Carries your bags and never tracks mud in your room."

"High Steaks," Alex suggests, staring into the horizon while writing calligraphy in the air with his hand, holding his cigarette.

I give Alex a concerned look. "You sure you didn't find those cigarettes from the Bardok party site as well? Plus, we don't serve steak."

"Yes, but that's the magic of it. Keep the guests wondering. Is there a clown? Do they serve steak? Who is the good looking man operating the grill?"

"The name needs to be simple. Also, you're not operating the grill again. You burned the food the last five times you cooked. And that's while being sober."

"Burned? I like my meat to be done when it's done. Besides, a little charring is good for flavour."

"A little? The meat was completely black and some of it was on fire."

"Oh that. That was one time. And I learned from my mistakes. No more drinking contest with Filip while on cook duty. In my defence, I won that contest."

I raise my beer and make a toast toward the fire pit. "Pork Paradise."

Filip laughs, his voice coming from behind me as he approaches from Vitali's house. "You trying to come up with names for food stand or just remembering your past relationships? I just checked the refrigerator. Just call it 'Pork and Pickles' and be done with it."

I look at Alex. Alex looks at Filip, then back at me. We both shrug. "Better than 'Clows in Mirrors' or what the fuck we had. Filip, go get a large piece of cardboard or some plywood. We have a name," I say victoriously. The burned out bonfire gives me an idea. "Alex, you go start the potatoes. All of them. Get every pot you can find and use it. Boil them to level of almost done, like last time. There should be some resistance when poking with knife. But peel them before boiling this time, I have idea for the leftovers. We have two hours until the county fair. I'll fix us a sign. Let's just hope Oscar delivers on his promise." I dig in the burned out bonfire and grab a large piece of charcoal. In a matter of minutes, Filip comes running back with a piece of plywood.

"What did you need it for? I think I can get bigger one." Filip is holding a piece the size of a small coffee table.

I take the plywood sheet and examine it, bend it and hit it a few times. "Good for start, but think bigger. Much bigger." He runs back toward the house. I start scribbling a draft of the sign on the small piece of wood. Moments later I hear a loud cracking sound, some loud swearing and more rustling near the house. Suddenly Filip emerges, dragging a piece of plywood the size of a barn door.

"Blyat that's more like it. Did you rip the front door off the house? Vitali will have cold winter this year. Go get a handsaw and we're in business." I use charcoal to write our chosen name on the sign and saw it in half, leaving the other half for use as a makeshift standing menu. I call Oscar to bring over the food truck. We spend the remaining time getting food ready and in half an hour he arrives, revealing our new base of operations - a repurposed horse trailer. Thankfully the thing that Oscar rolled up with isn't the basic single horse box, but a double width retro-looking carriage. Still undoubtedly a horse box, though.

"Why does it say Pork and Pickle? Are we selling just the one pickle? How big is it?" Alex asks.

"Fucking smartass. Keep the guests guessing, remember. Besides, once they come close enough to read the sign, they're close enough to smell the food. Then, it's game over. One-zero to Lev."

We raid Vitali's pantry for condiments and seasonings and pack all the half-prepared food into the trailer. Oscar hitches it to our car and we both drive to the county fair. I start to feel the excitement of the fair. Serving food to complete strangers. There's something much more raw about running a food truck compared to working in a restaurant or fast food place. The people get to choose your food from a large variety of competitors with equally fast service, but every client that decides to choose to go with your offerings is a win, a conquest of every other local food stand that's present. I don't even wonder about the unfair advantage I have over the others for being the only one from out of town, as locals will more likely want to try out something new that's on offer. We arrive at the site and the mass of people rushing in and out of the fair is severely disproportionate to any food festival happening in my hometown. We roll onto the grounds like VIPs, as the area is normally blocked off to cars. Our spot is placed strategically at the far end of the event, as most people will always walk through the fair and only at the end of browsing decide which food they want to try out.

"Shit, Oscar really pulled some strings. I'm impressed." I tell the others in the car as I look at the location reserved for us. "We still have half an hour before the food stands open. Alex, you ready?" I ask my cousin in the front seat, visibly excited and vibing to the loud music in the car.

"Not problem. You prep, I cook. Just like last time." He takes a shot of vodka and passes it back to me and Filip.

"Filip, you work the counter. We have cash and card terminal both this time, so get ready for some fast action," I tell him sitting beside me.

"I was doubting before, but now I'm sure," Filip starts saying nervously. "You didn't make enough. Look at all these hungry faces." He looks around and observes the attention we are getting just by setting up.

"We have enough. Just remember to keep your snacking of our own food to a minimum. We will be here for a good few hours, so grab a plate once you get a moment, but leave some for customers. Davai, work mode on, comrades. Let's make some money." I take a quick shot of vodka, pass it to Filip and step out of the car into the hot sun.

A long makeshift street of stands and booths reveals itself on the long path from the town hall to the community centre. We are now located in the exact middle of town. The hot weather provides us with perfect opportunity to lure in customers and focus on our food. I quickly realise however, that we aren't providing any cold refreshments. Just another missed opportunity if we don't manage to put something together on the spot.

"Perfect spot, no? You will be selling food faster than you can blink," says the extremely proud Oscar stepping out of his car. "You let me know of anything you need. I bring right away."

"You don't happen to have some ice cold kompot would you? People will be dying of thirst in this weather, even if Alex doesn't burn the fucking meat to a crisp." I ask Oscar and spot the nearby Alex flipping me off as he lights his cigarette.

"Kompot, no. But I do you one better. Give me 15 minutes, I bring you your drink." Oscar jumps in his car and races off in an unknown direction.

Alex, me and Filip stand in front of the repurposed horse trailer and visualise the final product of our stand. "Well this is fucked. People will think we sell horse meat here," Alex replies with concern.

"Filip, set up the signs. Hang the name plate above the customer window and prop the menu on the side. We'll just have to make the visitors think about something else than horse, then. Quick, what's the opposite of horse?" I ask the two comrades.

"Cow?" Filip replies.

"Unhorse." Alex says with certainty.

"Thanks, guys. Enlightening as always." I quickly draw a pig snout and pickles on the menu. "Filip, hang the menu on the side, so it will pull focus away from the trailer."

We step into the horse box for the first time to check out the equipment provided for us. The thing has definitely been used for food preparation, although not very thoroughly cleaned. Some food splatters on the walls and oil stains on the floor is however an expected sight given the low price of zero that we paid for the use of this trailer. The inside is built up with professional grade kitchen equipment, including a gas grill with four burners. A long preparation area next to the customer window is equipped with all the necessary tools I will need for the duration of our cooking operation. Alex assumes his position behind the grill, sets all burners on maximum and starts the process of heating up the cooking surface.

"We have slight problem here, bossman," Alex tells me. "Unless we going to heat up the meat with the anger of our enemies, we have small problem." He flips open the cupboard below the grill to reveal the gas canister missing. Just a tube leading to the spot where the gas container should be strapped to.

"Well, this could slow us down slightly. Filip, you know what to do."

"Sure, but won't they close us down for selling raw meat?"

"What? Gas! We need gas! Run to the hardware store and get the smallest one they have. Me and Alex will prep what we can, but we won't be selling anything without warm food. Go!"

Filip starts running to the closest hardware store, about a kilometre away. This leaves us enough time to prepare the food. I unpack the multiple containers of meat and pickles. Alex takes the potatoes he prepared earlier and sets them up for the final cooking. I take out my large containers of salt and pepper. Several blocks of butter are laid out on the counter. Alex lays out the first paper plates for serving, along with tons of wooden forks and knives. Our most important and largest container sits in the middle of the workstation - a massive tub of mayonnaise.

I look around the fair and spot several other food stands already cooking, pepping and setting out tables on the grass beside them. The tension is starting, the desire to win starts to emerge.

"Why don't we have tables? Where the blyat everyone going to eat? Back home?" I exit the food trailer and examine the nearby allocated patch of grass set out for us. "This will not do. People need to sit and do shots. We need chairs and tables!"

"Just tell Filip to bring some from the hardware store."

"With what? Smoke signals? That debil lost his phone long ago. Let's hope Oscar has some better news."

Just ten minutes before the food area opens, Oscar rolls up with his red station wagon, bringing a massive container of kvass behind him, hitched to the car. "Perfect timing or what? Look at this masterpiece. Hundred litres of drink, cooling system already integrated, we the only ones at the fair with this kind of luxury."

"That is some impressive fuckery to make this thing appear out of thin air. Where you get this from?" I ask him. Alex looking from the trailer, visibly impressed.

"What you think we do here all this time? Watch grass grow? The whole island produces massive amounts of the stuff. We can talk numbers later, you just sell the stuff until dry."

"In this weather, not problem. We have other problem though. Tables and chairs. Any ideas? We opening in ten minutes."

"Leave it to me, I know someone in the community centre, she will surely lend some from there," Oscar replies calmly.

"If it's Oksana, don't mention I'm here. Otherwise we get kicked out and banned for life." Alex cautiously replies from the window.

"Don't worry about Oksana, she and the mayor no longer together."

"Looks like whole island knows about you and the mayor's wife," I say jokingly. "Fuck it, ask her to come too. We have enough food for all."

At the same moment Filip comes running with a gas canister, completely tired by the hot burning sun, having run a whole kilometre. Alex takes the container, plugs it to the grill and sparks it to light.

"Does anything fucking work in this horse stable?" Alex yells with frustration. "Oscar where you get this thing? Walls covered in shit, gas grill not working. We end up selling DIY meat kits to people at this pace."

Oscar gets in the trailer and takes out some tools. The sound he makes draws even more attention to our half-ready culinary operation. A minute later he comes back. "Give it a go.

The gas valve sticks sometimes. Try not burn it down. Is rental."

Alex jumps in the trailer, puts all burners on full and sparks the gas. A small explosion comes from the inside and suddenly a large flame rises from the grill. "We are in business, comrades! You better start operating fast if we want to feed anyone today, Lev."

"I never doubted you for a minute," I tell Oscar and jump in the trailer. "I'm going to cut the pork into smaller pieces and skewer this cyka so we can cook as fast as possible. Check that the fryer is getting heat, that shit will take lot of time before it's operational. Did you bring the potato peels?"

Alex whips out the potatoes and the peels he made earlier. I sprinkle the whole batch generously with salt and pepper and hand the bowl to him for cooking. At this time the county fair announcer notifies that the food court has been opened. The small gate is opened and people slowly start rushing in. Filip, still catching his breath, jumps in the trailer and sets up his station at the window. I pour out vodka for all three of us, we make a quick toast and take the shot. It's showtime. The menu on the side of our food truck simply says:

Food

-Shashlik with pickle

-Doublecooked potato

-Potato peel

Drink

-kvass

-vodka

I slice up the marinated pork that I made the night before. Pork, vinegar, salt, pepper and onion. Not as strong as I usually make it, but our limited time frame didn't allow for three days of marination. The smaller pieces of meat cook considerably faster and add more flavour from the grill. Alex cooks the onions on the same skewer as pork for added flavour. The pickles are simply lightly salted marinated cucumber, marinated in saltwater, blackcurrant leaves, dill and horseradish leaves. Goes well with food and equally well with vodka. Served as sliced on the plate. Potato peels are the easiest to prepare. Simply deep fry until golden brown and serve in a cup. The boiled potato is somewhat more challenging, as heating it up on the grill takes time and deep frying it is ridiculous. Alex gets the idea of cutting the whole potatoes in half and slicing the round edge off one side to make them cook faster on the grill. He brushes them with butter and cooks them until brown. The potato is served with more butter and salt and pepper on the side.

I get to prepare the first snacks as the people approach the window. Filip takes charge of dealing with the client's orders and questions, Alex behind me operates the grill as he vibes to the music playing on our radio.

The first few orders are all ice cold kvass, as we seem to be the only ones providing it on this hot spring day. In a matter of minutes after opening, Oscar appears with some tables and chairs, providing seating for the hungry and thirsty fair visitors. I quickly check Alex's cooking situation and find that the smaller pieces of meat not only cook faster, but also look more plentiful on a plate. I cut up some pickles for free samples along with pieces of shashlik to go around.

In a matter of minutes the first larger orders start coming in. First for shashlik, then potato peels and then all of them combined. Filip, who's in charge of operating the cash and card payments, also takes some time to announce the menu and its great flavours to the new customers.

The food prep area is busy like rush hour traffic. The grill is burning on full power since the moment it was lit and the fryer is constantly pumping out fried potato peels. Filip takes on the job of plating the food as Alex starts getting overwhelmed with the new orders coming in. The cold kvass dispenser is self-service and vodka-pouring responsibility I take on myself. It's a well oiled machine.

As more people approach our food stand, even more come close just to investigate what the commotion is about.

Soon a line of ten people appears in front of the window. Some coming just for the food, some to have a quick chat and a shot. I guess last night's promotion worked well.

Alex is working the grill as fast as he can, only coming over to the window for some shots with customers who bought us a round. Me and Filip have assumed the role of crowd interaction, as more people just want a picture and some even an autograph.

"Hey these crazy people want give more money than I ask for. What I do?" Filip turns to me with concern.

"Write 'tips' on a cup and put in on the counter. If they want to give more money than the price then is not our place to say no. Let's split it later and buy a beer or something."

"Looks like many of these people came just for you, Lev. You want to do a quick fan meetup or something?"

"They will get a chance once the meat is all gone. Shouldn't be too long considering the fucking rush we're having. Plus there's the concert later," I tell him. "Actually, I'll make some time right now. Why keep people waiting?"

We sell, prep and cook for another two hours with an almost constant queue in front of the window. The few moments there are no customers around, Filip takes on the role of promoter, running around with free samples, luring in more people. Some sit by the tables, ordering shots, which I take on the job of serving.

As the time nears 5PM, progressively more people flock to the food court. Alex is working double speed, pushing out cups of deep fried potato peels and Alex has had to stop promoting the stand as we are at production capacity.

"We soon have problem bossman," Alex says from the grill area. "Peels are running out, only few potatoes are left, meat looks like it will last only few more rounds. Unless we plan to serve shots of mayonnaise, we need to close soon."

"Not problem, let's strike out pork from the name and serve shots and pickle," I tell him. "Lots of those left. We have to be running out of hungry customers at this point anyway. Workday over, let them enjoy the evening."

I call Oscar and tell him to bring few bags of potatoes and more vodkas. In a matter of minutes he appears with the requested items and takes the opportunity to refill the kvass machine. We keep going for another hour, serving mostly drinks and zakuski. Progressively more people in the crowd seem to be walking around with our cups full of potato peels. The tables are constantly full of customers enjoying the company, chatting with the crowd in the kitchen. I peel the new potatoes and assign the fry chef to cook them.

"What we do with the raw potatoes?" I ask the Filip and Alex, as we didn't bring a pot or water to boil them in. "I don't feel like converting to a french fry stand any time soon."

"Save them, let's cook them later by the beach. Some herbs and throw them in the fire with some aluminium foil," Alex suggests, taking another shot by the grill.

"You want to slow down with the drink there, grillmaster? You still need to play bass later at the concert."

"Me? These hands were born to play. Five more shots and I'm ready for stage," Alex replies proudly, running the fryer with the fresh potato peels. "You maybe need to save your voice and talk less." He has taken on the responsibility of playing the bass in my band several times, as the regular player constantly keeps disappearing and then reappearing weeks later. Only thing is, Alex never gets on stage sober. His play style and stage presence however seems to improve considerably when he's a few drinks in.

Filip turns away from the crowds of people gathering by the food truck. "What brotherhood of serfs is this? We not going to eat five kilograms of potato on the beach, comrades. Just slice the potato like you make the peels and throw in fryer. Salt, pepper, mayonnaise. Good to go. Is like fries but is not. The crowd demand food."

"The gopnik raise a good point, Lev. We completely out of meat now. Give me a knife, I can finally utilise my CSGO skills here."

I hand Alex the second knife and we both pump out heaps of thin long strips of raw potato, fry them in the oil and serve as a large heap on plate with mayonnaise on the side.

Filip takes the job of fixing the menu and updating it with our new offerings. We manage this workflow for another hour until the ingredients completely run out.

I come to the window and address the remaining crowd near our stand. "Closing time, last round is on us." This seems to attract an even larger group of people to approach. We pour out the last shots and cups of kvass for free, make a big toast and thank everyone for coming. I announce the concert that's starting in a few hours and close the stand with a "sold out" sign on the window. We leave the horse carriage at the fair for Oscar to pick up later and make our way away from the crowd.

We exit the fairground and Filip whips out a massive wad of cash from his back pocket. "Who's up for drinks? I'm buying."

"I don't know about you two, but I'm going to hit the beach campsite, grab some better sleeping accommodation than Vitali's old couch. You can go hit the bar if you still feeling sober."

"Actually, a break sounds good right now. I can't feel half my face after all that heat," Alex replies. "Better cool it down by the beach with cold sea air before the stage lights heat me up again later."

We walk to the nearest bus stop and take the city line to the beach, while Filip still counts the stack of cash in his hand.

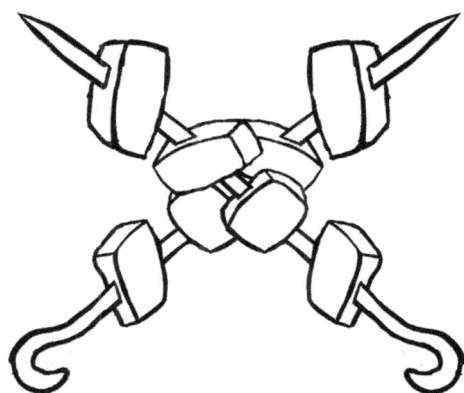

Part 8 - Stage

"I have to say, that was completely unfair to the competitors. Our stand sold out completely while other food truck owners were there standing like idiots looking at us like we invented fire," Alex says as we get off the bus at the beach.

"Hey, if they want to serve burgers and beer, let them serve burgers and beer," I tell him. "Others came here to make money, we came here to cook and drink. We just happened to cook for others, too. They probably need to do that shit every day and we here screwing with their business. But is just for one day, so I'm sure they forgive our guerrilla approach."

"So you knew others would be selling burgers?"

"No, I didn't even think about doing it before yesterday. I didn't know how many others would be there, if any. I was hungry and bored. I just went to cook some shashlik and have good time with the comrades."

Filip lights a cigarette as we approach the beach and starts getting strangely philosophical. "Food truck is one thing, but you perform concert today in new place to completely new crowd later. Most people are critics and assholes, you know. That don't bother you?"

"What? No. It's the complete opposite. As a matter of fact I only ever play for strangers. I never invite anyone I know to watch me perform. That's like putting on a show for your mama in your living room, showing her that you learned to juggle tennis balls at age of 25. If I could be anonymous so that nobody knew who I was, I would do that instead any day. What I do on stage should always be a standalone act and not corrupted by people's opinion of me in everyday life. When I'm on stage I'm just a fraction of myself. It's the most expressive of all the fractions of myself. And that's all that I need people to think about."

"That's one thing I don't understand," Alex says. "Most people have one job or do one thing. You work full time, do the food truck and the band thing. I wouldn't be surprised if there's a secret flower business you run in old town or something. Lev the friendly florist. Arrange flowers by day, scream in mic during night. You have three kids you pay alimony for or something?"

"I don't do it for money. Of course I wouldn't do everything for free, either. I do it because I get bored very easily. If I could do new thing every day I would."

"So why stop there?" Filip asks. "Go work in The Red Dog as bartender during the weekends as well. Masha would be thrilled to watch you bus tables all night."

"And serve you debils vodka while you talk about The Brown Hornet? I would not want to miss that for the world."

"White Hornet!" Filip screams.

"White, Orange, Blue, no matter now. That rust bucket is Sonya's problem. I doubt her and M even made it to the city with that car. They probably still on side of road, waiting for tow truck," I tell him as we sit down on the beach. "I'm making this my last performance. Don't tell anyone. Besides, the members are losing interest anyway and I have enough other things happening."

"The end of an era," Alex says while looking at the waves hit the beach with a steady roar. "Told you, Filip. Lev here has started a florist business."

"Actually I don't plan to return to city. I'll stay here for the summer, see where the road takes me."

"Bullshit. You done this shit twice now and always returned after a week," Filip starts with a distinct note of disbelief in his voice. "Alex, you remember the last time. We were here, sitting on beach by the fire and Lev started making plans to become airline pilot or some shit."

Alex starts laughing loudly. "Oh yes, Lev the levitation specialist. The ace of aviation."

"Fuck you debils," I tell them dismissively.

"Man, you just need to stop doing every fucking thing in the universe. Do one thing and see the world. Is what others do every day. Sure, you can get the high of feeling like superhero doing every job imaginable, but you never get to the good part."

"The good part? And what might that be, Alex?" I ask him.

"You won't believe me. It's called finding your place in life. You can find it in anything, but as long as you don't feel it, you haven't found it yet. And your place is definitely not on this sparsely populated distant island with a market that sells only one sort of onion. What's the plan? Farming potato here with Oscar and Vitali? You need to start doing something that doesn't require other people. People are assholes."

"Place in life? What fucking budget level late night psychology channel have you been watching? Just go pay for the fucking accommodation." I turn away from them as they walk toward the booking office, cracking jokes and laughing all the way.

I look at the sea and the evening sun high above it. The weather is hot, but a constant cool breeze keeps me at a comfortable temperature. A slight smell of seaweed hits my nose as I start contemplating my situation. Maybe they're right. I have been here before, stuck with a similar problem. Maybe it's the island itself that's making me lose focus of my goals, if I've ever even had any. This is a place for escape. It's all that it's ever been.

"Looks like we have good reason to cut the week short now. They even released the full lineup," Alex tells Filip in the distance.

"Can you buy me ticket, I pay you back once I pay for the thousand roses I need to get the wife once she realises how long I've been gone." Filip realises he still needs to get home and patch things up with his other half.

"What lineup? What?" I ask and turn toward them.

"Check your phone, patsan," Alex says and sits down next to me. "It's happening again. Bardok is running at full force. Shit, do you think they found my potatoes? OUR LOOT! I told you we should have taken more."

"You idiot, don't you see? That's why that stuff was there," I tell Alex "They probably planned the things weeks or months in advance. They stashed that shit away from debil raiders like you."

"Me? You the one who found the path inside. I was just there to sample the product. At least I know what I'm ordering this time."

"When is next time anyway?"

"Check the post. Saturday."

"Bullshit. Saturday this week? Blin, they really know how to promote urgency."

"No shit, they even got TenX as headliner again. Look at this lineup. They must have like 3 stages to fit all the artists in one day."

TenX is a notorious artist known mainly for his heavy distorted beats and anonymous persona. Ever since his appearance a few years ago, he's been playing in a wide variety of venues locally and internationally. Given the popularity of Bardok and the comeback vibe the event brings this year, I'm not surprised they got him to appear. It's by far the most popular artist there and also the reason we went to the event the previous years.

I check my phone and there it is - another Bardok party exactly as it was promoted two years ago. I get few more notifications but swipe them away. I can already guess what they are. Not going to deal with that now.

"I'm calling M, making reservations at the toolshed," Alex says victoriously. "Filip you look for another broken down car to sleep in as usual? Lev, I'm guessing you booking Sonya's cottage?"

"I will figure something out. Besides, I didn't get her number."

"I can ask M. I'm sure they hanging out."

"That's alright. Something tells me I'll be seeing her there."

I grab my bag and we make our way to our houses. The accommodation they booked consists of three small cottages further down the beach, in the small forested area with tall pines growing above. The ground is covered in a mix of sand and tons of pine needles. This is the third time we have been camping here. Even though the environment is very relaxing and what I have been looking for for days now, I still can't shake the feeling that I'm missing out on something. These are the pines, these are the juniper bushes I've been thinking of. But I can't think of anything else besides my next goal. I can't relax. Maybe vacationing is just not a thing I can do.

"Alex! How do I relax?" I ask him straight with a strict tone.

He looks at Filip. "Look, this is a man who has it all figured out," he says sarcastically and turns back to me. "You don't. *You* have a concert to give in an hour, you have people that depend on you. If you relax now, all goes to shit." He takes a drag from his cigarette. "At least that's what your brain thinks. You have been brainwashed into thinking you need to do a thousand things to survive. And even more things to make enough money to 'be someone'. I'm surprised you haven't cracked the code yet. You say you don't do it for the money, but more money is what separates you from the rest. At the end of the day you're just a gopnik like us, sleeping on the beach. I don't question your ambitions because hard work and struggling seems to keep you in a loop that your brain understands." He takes the wad of cash from Filip. "How many heaps of this do you think you have stashed away in your bank account right now? Ten? Hundred? Thousand? Even with a million, you still need a purpose, a goal to strive for to feel fulfilled. And I doubt you seem like someone who wants to retire in his twenties."

"Money is for bills and food. And the occasional trip to the woods." I explain to him.

"I think you overestimate the cost of these trips. Unless you plan to book the whole island next time, I think you would be equally satisfied with just the salary your office job supplies. Shit, you could easily live off any of these incomes and be twice as wealthy as the average person here. Look at Filip for example," he says as he points at the guy sitting on the sand, staring up into the pines waving in the heights. "His biggest worry is how he gets back home this week. And he's the one of us that's married. He's figured out the game. He doesn't even know he's sitting next to a massive anthill."

"Well, you still need some objective. Some end goal."

"End goal? You planning to save the rainforest or something? None of us has an end goal. You just work the week to enjoy the weekend. That's why they're packaged to a convenient set of 52 each year. If you're unlucky enough to have more month at the end of your money you just go ask babushka for supplies and carry on. Now let's go. I still need to practise holding that bass. Your songs are a fucking nightmare to play."

"Hey Filip," I yell at the guy sitting in sand. "You coming for security or plan to feed the ants for the rest of night?" He jumps up, quickly coming out of his daze.

"Yes commander," he says with a salute. "I'll punch out all the debils who approach."

"See there, that's a man of pure commitment. He does the job for free and he's happy for the opportunity. As long as the job is forcing vandals into submission, Filip has always been the man of choice." Alex stands up and goes to do a bit of mock fighting with the upcoming security guard.

I take a moment to sit on the bench in front of the houses and allow the words of wisdom to find a place in my head. I strike my hands together and make a loud clap, then stand up. "Alright. Let's go play some music!" I drop my bag off at the house and we make our way to the bus stop. I call Vitali and let him know of our approach and let his drummer brother prepare for our arrival. It has always been somewhat of a common occurrence to swap out band members at the last moment. This has never been much of an issue since most of the songs are known among the locals and playing them is somewhat a part of learning an instrument. Alex has helped me out in this area so many times that he's basically part of the band already and has no problem taking over the part of bass or second guitar. Since the start I have always been surprised at the simplicity of starting a band, it is however the part of keeping it going that's the hard part. I remember suggesting to many friends, relatives and acquaintances to start doing the same thing, as for me the whole process came somewhat easily. It seems that my words have never really sounded very true, as none of them really came through with starting something of their own. Or maybe they did and just didn't get very far and never mentioned to me their attempts. That's one of the problems with trying to inspire others. It's only the top one percent of their success that gets revealed to you and the general public. On the contrary there are probably many people who have attempted and failed, but I never get to see the part that really touches me the most - the struggle of starting. Perhaps it is the same issue that's keeping me from staying with my long term commitments and keeps me looking for another new challenge. I'm more interested in proving to myself that I can start than keeping something going for money and fame. Alex was right about one thing, having things figured out is only a point of perspective. There is no real "end goal" to speak of. I remember having a vision in my head of people learning and knowing our songs, as that would mean I have reached the ultimate goal. But as I went along, the priorities dynamically shifted toward something else, something that's even more impossible to achieve. The whole point of starting is to prove the point that makes you achieve it. Success is a point in time and not a challenge you're supposed to raise each time you reach the level you reach that you set out to reach.

We take the bus back to the county fair and meet with Vitali and his drum-playing brother in front of the community centre, where the stage has been set up. We get confirmation that we're going on at 9PM sharp. They hand us our loaner instruments for the evening - a fairly worn out Stratocaster for me and a significantly fresher Yamaha bass for Alex. We have a quick chat with the brother and trust his knowledge of my songs and his skill to replicate a sound that's close enough to the original style of the band. After confirming the best known songs to play from the repertoire of the drummer, we confirm the agreed upon short setlist of four hits, as that's how long the window for our performance today is. We agree to skip the practise and play it as it goes, only going through the details with the sound engineer. That's a common downside of doing a performance on last minute notice, but at same time the benefit of performing songs that are commonly known among professionals.

Vitali has managed to let the organisers squeeze us in as the first performance. This is a great benefit for us as we could get on stage early and take some time getting things in place without letting people wait too much between artists. As we get on stage and do quick sound check, I am surprised at the level of accuracy that Vitali's brother has achieved in tuning the instruments and amps for my sound. But it's also somewhat expected given the lack of experimental effects in the chosen tracks. I give the brother a thumbs up. Sound engineer confirms and gives us a green light.

"How's it feel, Alex?" I ask my cousin as I turn to him. "Looks like thousand people at fair. Better not freeze up."

Alex laughs dismissively. "Let's blow the roof off this cyka!"

I address the crowd, screaming into the mic. "We are '99 Below'. Inspired by the temperature of your ex's heart." The drummer counts us in and I play the opening riff to 'The Face To Face'. Alex follows, playing the bassline. Vitali's brother keeps the pace on the drums. Me and Alex take the opportunity to have a quick guitar battle in between the vocals. Progressively more people start to gather in front of the stage. I quickly check Filip and his security efforts, but he's on top of his task with dedication. I spot the low evening sun start to set beyond the city's buildings, but quickly get my focus back on track.

We play all four songs back to back with no big problems or interruptions, if not counting the time the drummer lost one of his mallets near the end of a song and had to play with his hand. We thank the audience, give a quick congratulatory handshake to the drummer and leave the stage, where we are met with the next artist. They're a local band that Vitali's brother plays for. We leave the instruments with the brother, who we only now thought to ask the name of - his name is Kristof. He tells me to keep the Strat, but needs to take the bass back as it's their backup instrument. I accept the gift and we wish him luck with his career.

"Blin, you always get the best shit," Alex says as we walk away from the event. "All I got was more calluses on my fingers from those cheap bass strings."

"You start doing vocals and the best shit starts running your way. Besides you can have the Strat. For a job well done. I'm sure this wasn't Kirstof's grandfather's first instrument or something."

"You lucky you got anything," Filip says walking slightly behind us. "All I got was a few elbows to the ribs and my toes stepped on. Was a good workout though."

"Lev, you said you not doing anything just for money but not for free either. Did they even pay you for the performance today?"

"Yeah, Vitali mentioned they're managing the payments next week. I'm guessing that's when the rest of the food truck cash should be arriving too, from the card terminal payments."

"So here is my question," Alex starts. "Would you have done the concert for free?"

"In this case? With people paying for entry and there being funding from the city - everyone gets money. It would have to be some charity show that gets paid with smiles and claps that would be completely free. But you wouldn't catch me playing there any time soon."

"So the case is closed. Lev is a dirty capitalist," Alex says proudly and lights up a cigarette and Filip laughs. "Did you see the massive crowd in the front row though? I was expecting maybe five people to show up." Alex is getting excited after the show ended fifteen minutes ago.

"Not too bad. There was definitely interest," I start explaining. "Never possible to know who came for which artist in these concerts."

"Nooooo no no they ALL came for me. I mean us. Some definitely came for Filip too, but maybe just to punch him out for standing in the way."

"Hey, they kept away because of the uniform of authority. Look at these long stripes running down the sleeve.

This is pure class." Filip points to the decoration on his tracksuit.

"If that's the worker's uniform I would like to see what the commanding officer looks like," I tell him.

We walk to the bus stop, sit at the bench and wait for the bus back to the beach. I was expecting to be dead tired after all the day's activities, but I feel the exact opposite. I don't feel like going to the beach and wait for the sun to set. I don't feel like ending the day. I feel like going back on stage and doing another full show. I quickly realise it's my never ending need to prove something that's keeping me going. I can't even remember the last time I went to sleep without being dead tired or drunk enough to pass out. This can't be what normal people feel.

I stand up from the bench and turn to the others. "What are we doing?"

"Oh no. Lev's at it again." Alex looks around. "Who gave him the reality pill this time?" he asks the invisible crowd around us. "What is it this time?"

"We should be doing something. Something big."

"We are. We going to sleep on the fucking beach. Or you talking about Oksana? I mean I can give you her number, but…"

"Feels like we forgot to do something. Something big. What am I forgetting?"

"I mean, we could get some fireworks and blow them up, but I feel there are better ways to spend money than watching coloured gunpowder burn in the air. You alright? You look a bit hyper." Alex looks very relaxed compared to what I'm feeling at the moment.

"Not that. I feel like a big day like this needs a big end."

"That's just the adrenaline talking. I tell you, you need to blow some shit up and you'll feel better. The high of today's row of success of activities can only be finalised by something equally big."

"Get me an axe," I tell him. "I need to cut down a tree."

Alex pauses and looks at me. Picks his phone out of his pocket and without asking any further questions calls Vitali. He arranges him to pick us up and take us back to his cottage. Some minutes later he arrives as. He was attending the concert at the time, but decided in favour of Alex's proposed plans. He picks us up and takes us back to his cottage on the other side of the island. The sun still lighting the spring day shows hints at us of a whole hour of daylight. Vitali, without asking any questions, hands me a woodcutting axe from the shed and takes a few steps back.

I take the axe and look at the trees in his yard. "Which one?"

Vitali points at the low pine tree growing in the far end of his yard. "Go crazy." Him, Alex and Filip each grab a lawn chair, light a cigarette and sit back to watch the show. "Should we be worried? Didn't he have like five shots at the food truck?" Vitali quietly asks the others.

"Lev? For him that's nothing. He's most probably stone cold sober at this point," Alex says. "He does this every once in a while."

"What? Go crazy?"

"Well, he's always been a bit crazy. I'm talking about the trees. For all I know he's a lumberjack in his free time and likes to practise. He never tells us. Honestly we have no idea. But the show is a spectacle."

I approach the tree. It seems old and dying. Nothing that would be missed and most probably needed to be cut down a while ago. I grab the axe and visualise the first hit, then take it. The axe hits the tree in the lower part of the trunk. The remaining stump would make a great seat or a small table. I try not to think about it. I hit the tree a few more times, landing each blow right in the previous spot. Small chips of wood start flying from the trunk as I get more hits in. Then progressively larger. I hardly notice as I get halfway through the dead tree and start hitting it from the other side. The axe feels sturdy in my hand, the tree is no match for each strong blow from the tool. I make a progressively stronger blow to the same place, pulling the axe back and swinging again. The tree is weak and fragile, but still puts up strong resistance. I land a few more blows and the tree falls down into the garden, missing all other trees and bushes. I look at the fallen pine and the trunk that remains. I'm not done yet. I start cutting off the bigger branches from it, then the smaller ones until just a bare trunk remains. I wipe my brow and throw off the jacket that's making me hot. I proceed to chop the trunk in half and then each in half again, then roll them into a pile along with all the branches and chips. I take a seat next to the others nearby.

"Good," I tell the others as I nod my head. "Better." I grab a beer from the case they have brought from the house. "Vitali you mind if we stay here again? The beach didn't work out."

"Stay for whole week. Maybe tomorrow you want I give you the chainsaw? Move faster."

"Faster?" I ask with confusion.

"You just spent two hours doing what looked like an execution on that tree. With chainsaw you can do ten trees in an hour."

I quickly check the time and realise it's midnight. The sun has completely gone and what lights the garden is just a flood light near the house. I had not noticed the passing of time in the heat of the moment. "Yeah. Maybe. Thanks." I take a look up and see a perfectly clear sky. The others continue their previous conversation beside me, as I lay on the lawn recliner. Pines. Yes, a strong smell of pines finally fills the air.

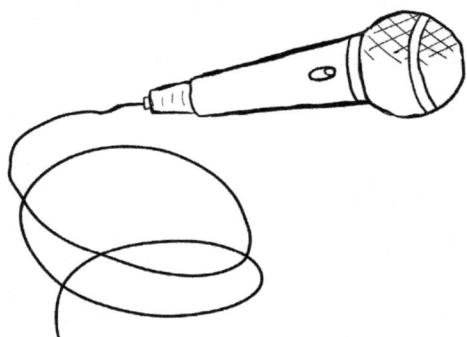

Part 9 - Palace of culture

I wake up. I once again realise I fell asleep in an unplanned spot. I have to stop doing that. Alex walks up to me with a cup of coffee and sits on a chair next to me.

"I'm going to skip the 'Alice in Wonderland' speech with you, as I know you're smart enough to see through it. But I am going to tell you something."

"I don't want to hear it," I tell him, rubbing my head, trying to clear my head from the perfectly good sleep I had under the clear sky.

"Probably not, but you need to."

"Was it that bad?"

"Actually the fight with the tree was very entertaining for us all. I'm talking about the general aimlessness you're experiencing again."

"Again?" I ask agitatedly.

"Yes you do this from time to time, you overwork yourself with ten different things and still keep searching for something more to keep you busy. Maybe from experiencing reality too much. I don't know. Everybody feel what you feel from time to time, but usually just for a moment after heavy night of drinking when the hangover makes us want to run head-first into a tree. What *you* experience is being lost."

"Lost? What samogon have you been drinking?"

"Lost is normal, we all feel lost. We feel lost because the world around us is lost. Look at this place - a relic stuck between past and present, both pulling with equal force. Many people lost their careers and goals once the Soviet Union collapsed. Some people mask their lack of objective in an endless search for something higher. Thats you. And you didn't even grow up in Soviet times."

I hold my head in disbelief of what he's talking about. "What?" I say monotonously.

"Others embrace the disorientation and go where the world goes day by day. That's Filip for example. His lack of goal in your eyes might seem like a life wasted, but his simple approach makes room for simpler pleasures. He simply a simple gopnik. He's just living. Either way, we are all wandering the same path." He lights a cigarette and takes a drag, crosses his legs and becomes progressively more philosophical, as I have known him to become after being sober for too long. "Unfortunately, what you're feeling is correct. To question it is natural. But the reason you haven't found the answer is because you're asking the wrong question. It's not what's the purpose, it's why we are looking for purpose in the first place.

"It's like when they say your body want to understand but your brain refuses to believe that the best way to enjoy life is to live it. Reality is hard to live for some because the present moment is happening all the time. It's like having a narrator for your life who's screaming 'NOW!' to you every three seconds. That's why so many people live in the past and use the present only to summarise what has already happened. You know those old guys sitting on park bench saying how good it used to be. It gives them the feeling that they're in control, but in reality they just blowing smoke. We've had this conversation before, you know. Don't worry, as long as I'm around I will happily nudge you back on the right track." He gives me a strong pat on the back and then takes a sip from his coffee.

"Fine, cousin. I agree some of that actually does sound familiar. I feel stupid now."

"That's just your brain finally understanding itself," Alex replies and stands up. "It's the morning talking. What I'm saying is you need a goal. Something that can only be achieved over time and not in one day."

I shrug and look at him. "Any suggestions?"

"You could start doing photography sessions in old town for tourists, then work yourself up to work for the newspaper."

"Oh is that all?" I ask sarcastically. "Why not become the next headliner at Bardok."

"How about start with something more realistic like starting a rice farm in the desert?"

"Let's keep working on it." I stand up, stretch and look at the mess I made with the axe last night. I point at the pile of lumber in the middle of the yard. "Few more of these and we have new bonfire."

"Now there's a man with a plan," he says with excitement. "Let's clean out Vitali's garden of the dead trees and make a fire at the beach later," Alex suggests. "What you think, Talik?" he yells across the yard toward the house.

A small window on the side of the house flies open and Vitali pokes his head out. "As long as I'm invited. I bring the sausages, deal?"

"Make it sausages and a case of beer and you got a deal. We working hard here after all," I tell him.

"Deal! But please, Lev. For sake of neighbour's sanity, use chainsaw this time. Also, I have work today, but you feel free with the deforestation project." Vitali closes the window and heads to his car, jumps in and drives off.

"Who he think we are?" I say as I look at the car driving away. "Ten minutes and we got this garden cleared out. Alex, get the chainsaw." I go in the house and make a new pot of hot coffee, greet Filip inside watching TV and ask him to join us outside for the woodcutting. I grab the whole pot of coffee and a large mug and head outside. We refuel the chainsaw and start the garden clearing mission. We cut down all the dead and rotten trees growing in the yard and pile them all in the centre for later pickup. It takes us no longer than 30 minutes. "Let's hit the city for some food, I'm starving."

We put away the chainsaw and start making our way toward the closest bus stop. Being roughly a four hour walk from the city, we choose to rather risk waiting for a local bus that hopefully runs on workdays than running that marathon. After a short ten minute walk we arrive at a bus stop bench on the side of the road that passes through the forest. The bus stop seems to be fairly fresh and at least maintained in this century. We look around the stop for any sign of the local line or a timetable of any kind, but no luck.

"I don't know about you comrades, but I could eat a whole ton of pelmeni right now," I tell the others.

"You not cooking tonight? I thought you had promised to pick up the whole pig and roast it on fire at the beach," Filip replies.

"Only if you want to wait eight hours and baste it every sixty minutes. Maybe next time. Let's get some potatoes, sausages and onion. Slice the onion and sausage and poke it on a stick and hold over fire. Throw potatoes in the fire in foil and dinner is ready. Salt, pepper, mayonnaise - is all we need."

"Throw in some tomatoes too," says the Alex leaning against the bus stop sign, smoking a cigarette. "I feel I'm thinning after having shashlik and vodka all day. Grab a new pack of cigarettes, too."

"Sounds good," I tell him. "Now all we need is an amp for the guitar and we sorted with entertainment as well."

"I got it covered," Says Alex, blowing a puff of smoke.

"What do you mean you got it covered? You going to plug it into the sand and wait for thunder to strike?"

"Is ok, I got it covered."

I look at him hesitantly. "Okay, Alex will make an amp appear out of thin air and also a fifty metre extension cord to run from the house. Good. I will get the ingredients for dinner from the market and Filip will go grab us something to eat right now from the store. Let's meet at the community centre park."

A small loud bus appears from around the curve of the countryside road. We get on and pay the driver for our tickets. The few people on the bus greet us as if we were old friends. The benefit of living in a small community. We strike a conversation with the local villagers who are going to the city to pick up groceries and we talk about life on the island. We arrive in the city, say goodbye to the locals and make our way to our individual objectives. I start making my way to the market and observing the slow life of the town, realise I couldn't fit in here if I tried my hardest. I have been living in the capital city my whole life, surrounded by a large variety of life of every kind. The people that get to live in an idyllic environment like this, first of all don't think of it as idyllic in the first place and secondly have been living here most of their life. They simply couldn't imagine living elsewhere, most of all in a large city, due to the irritating high strung lifestyle and alleged high crime rate.

Shortly after setting off, I realise I have been alone for no longer than a few minutes during the entire trip. My epiphany is overshadowed by the sudden and nearly instant arrival of ominous dark clouds that block out the sweltering sun. The sky falls open and the pavement, desert-dry only a minute ago, overflows with a swell of rainwater. The heat from my path must have warmed the cool rain to a near boil after having accumulated hours of the intense spring sun. A monstrous roar that the millions of raindrops make surround me in an invisible wall and what plan I had to keep walking is instantly replaced by the overwhelming desire to allow the torrent to drench me completely. I reduce the pace of my forward movement to a slow wander and watch as the remaining pedestrians occupying the street hasten their pace to account for the sudden change in meteorological conditions. Never have I understood people's obsession with staying dry in rainy weather. Are wet clothes uncomfortable or are people just embarrassed to be seen in them? I disregard the thoughts and continue my walk at a leisurely pace.

The market salesmen seem to not be bothered by the weather change. They actually visibly enjoy the change from the hot temperatures that have been exhausting both the people and the freshness of the picked produce. I select what goods I came for and leave the market. Getting closer to our planned meeting place at the community centre, I quickly realise others are possibly not as intrigued by the downpour and will be delayed considerably. As the idea of standing in the progressively colder weather seems unappealing, I go inside the community centre and leave my jacket to dry in the coat check room, along with the bags of goods from the market.

Observing the long halls and high ceilings of the centre, I am greeted with a strange familiarity of similar places I have visited previously. There is a distinguishable style in common with other community buildings like the wooden decorations and elaborate use of balconies and mezzanines. Commonly also known as palaces of culture, many similar buildings around the country used to serve a similar purpose - to prevent the working class from falling into a cultureless life of drinking. Now these massive blocks of concrete have almost completely been repurposed as libraries, cinemas and rentable rooms for hobby groups.

Walking through this seemingly ancient piece of architecture, I get hit with the smell of old linoleum that has been warmed by the sun. There is also the unquestionably clear aroma of old cloth-covered chairs and the wood they're made of, which has undoubtedly started to show its age.

I can only imagine the organised events that took place here and their tremendous importance at the time, both socially and politically. Even more so, the equally immense consequence of not attending an event in case of changed opinions about the state.

Having not lived during the Soviet times, I only have stories and history books to base my understanding on, especially about events happening in the 60s and 70s, where the rule of the USSR loomed over every citizen unfortunate enough to be living in it. The percentage of people living in unforgivingly harsh conditions, compared to anyone who frequented a house of culture, must have been massive, even considering the amount of these purpose-built establishments across the countries under Soviet rule. Big ideas being discussed by old men with tremendous plans, only to be filtered down to simple words that the population can understand and read on an eye-catching propaganda poster on the street.

The amount of times I have heard someone born in the Soviet times talk about how much better things used to be is comparable tenfold to the amount of those that complain about how much the opposite was true. It seems like an effortless struggle to understand anyone not living for the future or at least the present. I'm starting to realise Alex might have a point.

The sheer amount of people living among us that had to cope with the new age of post-Soviet life must be feeling ten times as lost as I am. Industries changed, workforce was reallocated in a completely new manner and education became something you have to hope for and is not guaranteed with the right choices. The modern world is still catching up, at least in this part of the world.

The community centre's main entrance swings open and my self-guided tour of this relic is cut short by two debils carrying large bags of food and a massive briefcase.

"What the fuck, Lev?" Alex yells. "Why you not hit market yet, make another crysis in local food supply?"

I quickly realise that the time I have wasted internally admiring this decorated concrete block has given the other patsans the opportunity to finish their tasks. "What's in the briefcase? Looks like accordion from antique store."

"This is our entertainment tonight. What you doing in this government palace? I can't be seen walking around here," Alex says quietly, looking around himself.

"You still worried about Oksana? I'm sure she forgot you already by now. Oh look she's coming right now." I point toward the hallway behind Alex.

He drops his briefcase in panic and looks behind only to see nobody there besides the coat check worker. He quickly turns back to me, shakes his fist in anger and walks out of the building.

"Oh come on!" I yell at him as he swings open the door. "How else I keep myself entertained?" I laugh and run to pick up my drying jacket and the bags filled with produce from the market. The door is left open behind them and the chalky smell of drying asphalt greets me as I step outside. "Mmm. Paradise." The rain has already stopped and is yet again replaced with a moody overcast, characteristic to the venue I just vacated. Alex and Filip seem visibly tired from their tasks.

"I tell you Alex, this man has life figured out," Filip starts. "Goes to community centre, walks out with gifts from the local babushkas." He points at the bags in my hand. "For some people life just comes to them."

"Some people just work and don't wait for money to appear from clear sky while smoking on balcony," I reply. "When you getting a job, huh?"

"And miss all this? Never." Filip pulls out a bottle of vodka and we all cheer from the excitement the evening on beach will bring.

Part 10 - Dacha

We once again take the city bus to the beach and make our way to the housing we planned to use already the day before. They are three small dachas side by side, only a few metres apart. Actually calling them cottages or beach huts would be more suitable as they serve to sleep only two people on their single storey. The inside has a strong smell of hay and lumber, presumably from that being their main building material. The windows are small and their frames are decorated with intricate engravings both inside and out. Each house has two single beds with spring mattresses that squeak loudly every time you make the slightest move on them. The small wood burning stoves that clearly had been originally built in them, have been replaced with a small kitchen corner and hotplate. This is presumably due to the temporary occupants being careless with making fires for cooking and not taking into consideration the flammability of the old wooden house. That is confirmed by the fact that the fourth house in our row has been replaced with a pile of ash and charred logs. However, this can be argued to be the work of vandals who commonly set houses like these on fire just for fun, when the buildings are not in use during colder periods.

We unpack the food that Filip has bought from the store and set up our lunch on a small table I borrowed from my cottage. The plastic bags reveal a feast of meat-filled piroshki, doctor's sausage, pickles and black bread. I pour out some vodka into the small cups from the house and we make a small toast. "To the bus driver who got us here safely."

Alex stands up. "To Vitali for letting us sleep at his house for the low price of a bonfire."

Filip follows. "To the vodka and may it never run out!"

I stand up and raise my cup. "To Alex's world-class mechanic skill that brought back to life the Red Hornet."

Alex raises his cup even higher and screams "to the Red Hornet!"

Filip takes out the wad of cash he got from selling his car and smacks in on the table. "Call it what you want, without that car we would not be here."

A short pause. "To Filip!" scream Alex and me. We hit our cups together so hard that some of the vodka inside them sloshes out, take our shots and start the well-deserved lunch.

People walking on the beach take notice of our festivities. The shoreline runs only 50 metres from the houses after all. I wave to some of the people to join us and it takes no more than a few attempts to make our company grow from three to six. The additional people who join turn out to be working on a local farm. We talk about life on the island, the weather and Ladas. No small talk. Just big ideas. Then spend three more hours taking shots and singing old time folk songs. The strangers, whose names we never asked, leave and continue on their path.

"You know you're the only person I know who would ask complete strangers to join us and start a conversation about shit that actually has a point," Alex says, slouching on the table after consuming a generous amount of potato juice.

"I had ulterior motives. They are the crazy ones for revealing such classified details as 'life here is shit'. We know this. Life is shit everywhere. Life is like a long conveyor belt of manure going round and round at a cow barn. The longer you live, the more shit you see."

Alex pours another shot. "And then we have more vodka, forget the old shit and start new day fresh." He raises his cup and we toast to our health.

A red station wagon rolls up behind the houses. I whistle at the driver and wave him over.

"Not more comrades, Lev. I have had enough social interaction for one year," Alex complains to me.

"Is just Vitali. He brought us firewood for cooking. Look!" I take a cigarette from Alex's pack and light up.

"Looks like vodka finally took my eyesight, because I'm seeing three people walking over here," Filip says as he's squinting to see more clearly.

"Well, shit," I say as I blow out a lungful of smoke. "Alex, you know something about this?"

He looks at me in disbelief. "Me? Noooo. The world works in mysterious ways." He jumps up and runs toward the approaching people.

It is undoubtedly Sonya and M that have arrived with Vitali. Sonya smiles at me and walks toward our table. "I never got your number," she tells me in a friendly complaining voice.

I lean back in the chair, doing my best to remove the expression of surprise from my face. "You never asked."

Alex grabs M and runs toward the water, her laughing and screaming along the way. They run into the waves, fully clothed and drop in the water.

"Mila didn't want to come alone," Sonya says. "Alex invited her some days ago. He arranged Vitali to pick us up from the port."

"So, she has a name." I do my best to sound like I hadn't just downed six shots of vodka. My attempts to focus on the person right in front of me must seem to a bystander like a massively challenging task. "I saw the event announcement for Saturday. I assume you're going."

"You could say that." She's doing her best to sound oblivious to the fact that she's the main organiser of the event, but I quickly disregard Filip's attentiveness from the conversation as he seems even less conscious than usual after a good drinking. I make my way to Vitali's car to unload the logs of pine. With the help of others around I carry all the burnable material to the beach and we light the bonfire for cooking the upcoming feast. I sit by the fire near Sonya, making sure to distance myself from others not being in earshot.

"I heard you had a concert," she says, warming her feet by the bonfire.

"It's no Bardok, but is life. Good crowd, many fans for this small place. I bet a good deal of them came from the mainland."

"Sorry I couldn't get you into the lineup again."

"Phah! To perform alongside all those digital debils pressing play on their laptop and jumping for an hour? I think I will survive. I'm more interested in why you left the promotion to the last minute."

"Actually the whole event idea came to me on Monday."

"Bullshit. This Monday? These things take months to prepare. But I guess when you own the venue and invite recurring artists, the preparation is easier."

"Honestly I just got lucky. Most of the vendors and crew were excited to do an event this quickly. Those who couldn't come on such short notice, I got to replace with alternatives. I just used the same platforms and contacts that I used before. If anything, I just wanted to see what the outcome would be."

"Well, you still can't choose the audience. Most people have plans for weekends."

"Actually the ticket sales reflect a similar attendance as the last event. I guess the sense of urgency and exclusivity provided much curiosity."

"Blin, why even do anything in advance then?" I ask her in disbelief. "They should announce the Olympic Games two days in advance as well, catch everyone equally off guard."

"If the organiser owns the venue, I don't see why not. I would love to watch that show."

"And now approaching: the runner from Nicaragua," I yell in an announcer's voice. "And he seems to be still wearing the swimsuit he just went to beach with the day before! No hope for world record here, but the attendance is record breaking!"

She laughs and stares into the distance over the water.

"You really don't realise how unbelievable this sounds, you organising an event like this. At least we would have never guessed. I assumed it was some high up executives and people with powerful contacts who could arrange something like this."

"Well, that's the reason I kept it secret in the first place. People wouldn't really take me seriously if they knew I don't act as crazy in real life as the events are. I could never live up to it. Not to mention the fact that I'm the organiser."

"Really? I don't have that problem. I just live the same life on stage that I live daily. I would take a case of beer on stage if it didn't hinder my playing."

"This week's event is more of a 'right time in right place' type of situation. Since I get to host the event and provide much of the sellable drinks for vendors, I need very little outside help organising. Sure, there's managers of the service providers, but I get to choose what goes where and how things happen."

"Yeah I would not want to be in charge of cleaning up after those events. I'm surprised your house there is still in one piece."

"That issue I avoided fairly early. I just had to put up barriers that directed the foot traffic away from it. I also left the lights on so the party attendants didn't think it was some abandoned house to go exploring. No offence to your friend."

"Oh yes, the two bottles of drink we borrowed. I'm sure the visitors will find something else to consume."

"Actually, you finding those drinks gave me the idea. I was just storing them there for an unknown time, since I had no place to put them in the city. And storage fees for extended time make them cost more than they're worth when selling."

"In that case I will take my prize in form of a ticket, please," I tell her, placing my empty hand out in front of her.

"Oh didn't you hear? I was planning to provide free entry to you and your friends."

"I guess you were a bit too late, they already bought the tickets. Besides, they would get suspicious of where I managed to swindle free access to the party of the century. Actually, we're more curious about how you managed to get a headliner like TenX in such short notice."

"Don't get me started on that guy. I get the whole anonymous performance act but he replies as slow as a snail. He must have three managers who relay all his messages to him." She gets visibly outraged, presumably by the stress of organising the event. "But his music is good and people like him. And his only requests for backstage are water and a pair of black socks."

"Why socks? And why black? What if you bring pink socks? He just not go on stage?"

"It's not my place to ask. I have never even spoken a word with him in person. Everything is organised through emails by managers. He appears, plays, disappears."

"I almost forgot!" I suddenly remember what I wanted to ask a while ago. "How's the car? You ever make it back to city?"

"You're not gonna believe this. Actually your friend Filip would be a bit mad at me if he found out. I sold it."

"And the Blue Wasp rides no more!" I scream so loud it echoes through the forest and the beach.

"I got in contact with Vova on my way back to the city and explained my situation with his car. He must have felt bad about its condition and offered to buy it back from me. We managed to drive it back to the city to a garage he owns and left it there. He transferred the money the next day and that's the end. I still have no idea if it will even start next time."

Filip appears from behind the roaring bonfire. "Someone mention the car?"

"Sonya sold your old car to Vova and made a million from it. She's offered to buy you a ticket for Bardok party."

Filip stops in place. Gives me a thumbs up, looking visibly impressed, then backs away behind the fire from where he came.

"You see, it all works out." I get up, walk to the house, grab some potatoes, wrap them in foil and throw them near the fire in the hot sand.

The last few hours of the day we spend prepping, cooking and enjoying the food I bought from market. The sausages go on long sticks along with rings of raw onion. The correct placement near a steady heat source brings out both flavours and mixes them nicely. Since we have a fairly large fire to work with, we push the sticks with skewered sausages straight into sand, standing upright. I jokingly say it looks like a makeshift fence for keeping vegans away.

Alex takes out the large briefcase he brought from city and reveals its contents.

"I hope you not planning on getting on plane with this," I tell him, looking at the complex electronics running inside it. It turns out to be a homemade guitar amp with an extension cord running out of it. From the looks of it, someone repaired and repurposed some old gear and for the lack of better case, built it in here. Impressive, really.

Alex plugs in his new guitar and plays a series of songs for the rest of the night as we enjoy the bonfire-cooked food. I never even asked where he got the homemade amp from.

Part 11 - The Show

I wake up, realising once again I failed to find a bed in time. I'm already getting used to this. Why not throw bed out and fill whole bedroom at home with sand instead? A new sensation surprises me, however. A blanket has been placed on me while I was out. I take a quick look around and find Alex and M still talking next to the completely burned out bonfire.

"What time is it?" I ask them.

"Still early, go back sleep. It's 5 in the morning," Alex replies.

"No point wasting the whole day, blin," I reply and start walking toward the water. I take off my jacket, shirt and pants and run into the sea. The cold shock of the water wakes me up, but pushes me out of the water in minutes. I take my clothes and put on the blanket that was covering me earlier. I say goodnight to the two still sitting by the bonfire and head into my house.

"We put her up in your house," Alex shouts in my direction as I approach my accommodation.

I wave my hands wildly in protest. "Why? Why not Filip's house?"

"And allow Sonya to get mentally scarred by Filip's snoring? I think not."

I approach my dacha, swing open the door and spot a person in my bed. "Of course in my bed," I mutter to myself. The clothes land on the floor and I drop on the unoccupied bed, still covered in my blanket and fall asleep.

As I open my eyes, I am instantly met with an uncomfortable sensation of there being at least 50 degrees of warmth inside the room. "FUCK!" I scream and quickly get up and open the door to the outside. "Can't a person get one good night of sleep on this island?" I scream at anyone listening.

"And the crypt door swings open!" Alex is sitting in the exact location as he was when I last saw him, but this time sitting next to Vitali. Sonya and M sitting on the other side of the bonfire, which seems to be lit once again. Filip laying down on the sand, looking toward the sea. "Well good morning, Nosferatu. Good sleep?"

"Nosferatu is the name of the movie, debil. That's like calling someone Frankenstein." I have strangely failed to recover my voice from the sleep.

"Get the man some beer, he's talking sense again!" Alex screams, imitating a doctor.

I quickly realise I have forgotten to put clothes on, turn back, put on a towel from inside and head straight to the beach. Vitali throws me a cold beer and I make my way straight to the water to cool off from what felt like sleeping in a hot sauna. The water is strangely warm, as if having been heated up significantly after my last dip. The realisation of time of day starts to come to me. "What time is it?" I yell at the people sitting on the beach. They look at each other and utter something silently. After a few moments, Sonya stands up and walks toward the water, takes off her dress, leaving just the bikini underneath and starts making her way toward me.

"I guess it's that time," I say to myself quietly. I move to a significantly shallower depth since if she came to where I was standing, she'd be completely underwater.

"Lev," she says as she's almost completely next to me. "I didn't just come because Mila needed someone to come with. Actually it was me who planned to come in the first place."

I look at her in confusion. "That's not a time. Is there a broken telephone situation here?"

She laughs and replies "Alex told me you would say something like that."

"Was I in a coma or something? What's going on? What day is it?"

"Lev, It's 7PM. You were asleep for like 14 hours."

I scratch my head in disbelief. "That does explain the hunger. And the strangely clear head. What were you all doing for all this time?"

"Me and Mila went to the store for some food with Vitali's car. The others actually just got up an hour ago. I guess the fresh sea air works great for you."

"Not to mention the pines and junipers," I reply rubbing my eyes, still groggy from the sleeping marathon.

"You want something to eat? You look like you could use some food. Let me make you something."

"Wait, were you planning on sleeping in my house all along? Or you didn't think that far ahead?"

She blushes, smiles, turns away and starts walking toward the houses. Back at the beach, I sit down at the bonfire that has been refuelled for cooking another meal. Alex is grinning at me like crazy.

"Lev, always the smooth talker." Everyone laughs. I stay left in confusion.

"We still don't have transport for tomorrow to get to Bardok, not to mention getting home after," I tell the others.

"That sounds like a problem for tomorrow's Alex," the cousin replies. "Today we hitting the sauna."

"Now there is a bright idea," I say and point at Alex. "So what's the plan? Turn up the hotplate in my house and we all get in there? It must be like 60 degrees in there already."

"Maybe next time," Alex replies dismissively. "I contacted the host, the owner of these houses. He has a big dacha with sauna only a few kilometres from here. Only thing is, the house is on another island."

"How the blin we get there? There a bank connecting the two places?"

"Not worry, we going on his boat. He even offered to only ask for rent of house for few hours and not whole day."

As promised, the host picks us up an hour later and we make our way to the other island which is covered in a thick forest of pines. The house is a massive tsarist-era dacha with a significantly fresher sauna built in during the last decade. We heat the sauna, splash water on the hot stones on the wood-burning stove and take dips in the nearby sea. We make our way back to the main island as the sun starts going down.

Me, Alex, Vitali and Filip spend the next day driving around the island, doing a basic sightseeing tour that Vitali had suggested the night before. For what it's worth, there are definitely lots more trees here than in city, but in city there is at least a bum or gopnik on street corner to look and point at. I quickly conclude that the island life is not for me and take a beer, pass one to Alex and Filip and we make our way back to the beach. Mila and Sonya had stayed back at the houses, presumably to organise the last details of the event that is set to happen tonight. Seems like a foolish endeavour to not be present literally where the event is set to happen, but after a short explanation by Alex, I quickly realise I am an idiot. I know why she came, I just keep myself so busy with being myself that I give no time to thinking what others think. Especially not about me. If I started to think about what people think of me, I would never do anything outside of being home and watching television. I disregard the new information and keep enjoying the day that is set to end with the largest biggest party of the century.

As the day starts to show signs of ending sometime soon, we start making our way to Bardok, as the party is set to start at 10PM. Vitali, who has offered to drop us off, agrees to do so for the low price of a tank of fuel and ferry tickets from and to the island. We swiftly take him up on the offer and pack our things in the car. Vitali driving, Filip sitting in front, Alex sitting in the back with Mila on his lap and Sonya sitting next to me on the back seat. For a moment we consider throwing Filip in the trunk, as the station wagon's rear space is by far the most comfortable seat in the car, but Filip quickly declines on the count of there still being heaps of pine needles and twigs remaining from before.

As we are driving to the ferry, I quickly realise a harsh truth. I was never going to be able to smell any junipers or pines just by staying near them, as they're likely most fragrant in the hot sun after rain, which are already rare occurrences to come by, given the time of year. The illusion of nature smells is strongly amplified by memories of such things. The longer I sit in the pine-covered inside of the car, the more I realise that my memories of such aromas are based on going to watch my father work in the forest cutting trees and then transporting them. It's definitely pines and junipers that I remember. Maybe even fir trees during Christmas time, when we went to get one from the woods. But never have I really associated simple clean air with any scent. I guess I just needed to get away. Next time I will know.

We arrive on the ferry, buy our tickets and get aboard. I make my way to the observation deck to take one last look at the passing island as others wait in the car, observably exhausted from our adventure. The sun starts to set as we reach the mainland. Long streaks once again start to run across the fields that we drive past. The strong heat from previous days is now replaced with just a bright light and cool air. It is definitely still spring.

Large signs start appearing on the side of road as we near Bardok. Artist names, ticket prices, event times - all clearly visible along with something I had not realised before. For the first time the event has a title instead of the unnamed Bardok rave everyone called it. On the top of the posters, in clear bright colourful text, eerily similar to the packaging of the drinks we found in Sonya's barn, there is a text that simply reads 'Roadside Midnight'. I already know what's going on. I don't even mention anything to Sonya, who is now obsessively typing on her phone, presumably remotely organising the already started event. As we start nearing the venue, bright laser shows and smoke effects can be seen from where the main stage is located. Long rows of cars park along the road to the event. The field next to where Filip's Lada had broken down just days ago, has been converted into a massive parking lot. No free spots can be seen in the endless rows of cars. Sonya directs our driver to take a detour and drive around the fencing of the main entrance to the rear of the event. A security guard checks our car and allows us to drive to the restricted zone after Sonya checks us in. The whole area is yet again completely unrecognisable from what it is outside of the events. Large crowds, massive fences, loud music - all things that made me forget that there ever was a kolkhoz here. We park just behind the small house in which I had spent the night this same Monday and make our way inside. The whole place has been converted into a bustling hub of managers and organisers. The once dark building with no electricity and a small coffee table is now filled with tens of people running in and out, talking on phones and writing things down in laptops.

"You did all this?" I ask Sonya, who already seems to be in demand.

"I just know some people. As I said, it snowballed." Before she can continue with her conversation, a manager pulls her aside to talk about something that sounded like a press interview. "You go join the event, I'm needed here. I'll catch up with you soon," she tells us and points us to the staff entrance to the event, then gives us special passes for getting back to the organiser's area.

We show our passes to security and proceed to the inside of the fences. We are instantly transported from a thick forest to the middle of a busy makeshift street, filled with guests walking in both directions. Either side of the street is packed with food and merchandise vendors, small bars and information kiosks placed tightly next to each other. "This could not have been done in just five days," I think to myself, but soon realise I have no idea how events are organised in the first place. As amazing as the sight is, I could never imagine myself doing anything like this as a job, not even once a year as Sonya does. The chances of so many things going wrong with so many moving parts must drive anyone insane. I guess I can imagine why she quit doing it those years ago. But why start now again? And on such short notice.

We decide to split up, Alex and Mila take the path on the left, I go right and Filip just sits down at the small makeshift bar which is essentially a beer tap and a set of chairs next to a stall not much bigger than our horse box food truck. I make my way to the main stage and put on sunglasses from my bag as I get closer to the bright lights and lasers. The crowd around the main stage is packed full, making it nearly impossible to get through, but thankfully I only need to get to the sound technician opposite the stage, behind the crowd. I see my friend Tom operating one of the effects panels and we have a quick conversation. He is one of the few people that was guaranteed to be here, as he's working with a few of the artists in today's lineup. We talk about what's interesting to check out at the venue and I make my way around the stalls to get something to eat. I take my time as the headliner is set to go on in half an hour.

The food at the stalls is great. I grab a cup of deep fried pelmeni with sour cream and keep walking around the park, eating the delicious snack with a wooden fork. Realising I never got to experience junipers in any significant way, I also order a gin and tonic. After all, there are no problems on vacation, only solutions. I soon meet up with Alex and Mila, who I need to scream with to communicate, as we are that close to the main stage. We soon meet up with Sonya, who delegated her tasks to come enjoy the main stage artist. Remembering Filip's lack of communication device, I quickly go search for him around where I last saw him, but the bar does not have him in there. I return to the others and we decide that since there's no way to communicate with him anyway, to just meet up after the event at the house. It's now just five minutes before the headliner is set to come on, at midnight. Sonya starts getting visibly anxious about there being no movement on stage and getting notifications from the managers on her phone about the artist not having arrived yet. It's perfectly normal for bigger artists to make a sudden appearance or even run late some ten minutes.

"Something is wrong?" I ask Sonya, who I have to almost scream at to make any sound reach her besides the ten thousand people in front of the stage screaming 'TenX' in unison.

"He didn't appear," she says nervously. "He's always been present at least half an hour in backstage before his timeslot. I don't know what's going on. He apparently checked in, but hasn't showed yet. It could be a problem." She has to yell almost at full volume to make her words sound clear.

"HEY!" Alex screams. "What if Filip is TenX? Matches the description. Can't play instruments and is late all the time."

"Is he? He's your friend, maybe you can tell him to get on stage?" She asks nervously.

"Filip the fantastic? Hah!" I yell. "The man used a phone with numeric keypad and he lost even that. He's not the one you're looking for."

It's now just two minutes to midnight and Sonya is texting almost endlessly with someone, trying to shine some light on the situation.

"Sonya," I tell her. "This is by far the best Bardok party yet. Who came up with the name?"

She smiles. "I did. A kind stranger inspired it," she says, her eyes still glued to the phone.

"It's funny you should say that. It's about to get a lot stranger." I tell her and put down my bag. She looks away from her phone at what I'm doing. "Don't worry, I just wanted to mess with you. It's all good, I checked in with Tom in sound tech."

"What?" she yells. "What do you mean?"

"Sonya, I understand what you're looking for, but... I'm very, *very* busy." I pull out a mask, sunglasses and furry hat from my bag. "I would tell you to keep it secret, but who would believe you?" I put on the sunglasses and start running toward the side of the main stage.

Sonya's face drops, Mila stands in confusion and Alex starts laughing maniacally.

"I *knew* he was working too hard. That crazy cyka," Alex yells as the chants from the crowd become louder.

"He's..." Sonya starts saying, looking at Alex. "Wait, you didn't know?"

"That he wears sunglasses at night? It has come up a few times," Alex replies, still laughing.

A few minutes later the crowd starts screaming and clapping as smoke effects and red lasers make the scene for the starting show.

I press play.

Part 12 - City

I take off the outfit and throw it back in the bag as I make my way off the stage. The adrenaline still rushes through me as I pass the stage crew, flashing my performer's ID. Suddenly I appear back on the makeshift streets of the event, people rushing in both directions, nobody taking a second look in my direction. "And that's how it's done," I mutter to myself. "Why even do anything publicly?" Quickly I make my way to the festival area with the most bars, sit down and message Alex to join me. The cousin appears in few minute's time along with Filip and Mila.

"It all makes sense now," he says grinning, still having to raise his voice as the next artist has started playing.

"What? I was in bathroom."

"You might have a problem, you were there for an hour, but from your speed of running there, I understand." We both laugh and order a drink from the bar. Unsurprisingly we see the same vodka-flavoured drink on the menu that we found in the barn on Monday and I order four shots of it despite the bartender telling me it's meant to be consumed with pineapple juice.

"Where's the local?" I ask, seeing there is one member missing from the group.

"Sonya the spectacular? She had to run to the house. I think she works here now." He raises the glass and we take a shot toasting the event and celebrate the perfect end to the long week of living life.

We spend the rest of the evening checking out the numerous stalls and shops that were set up especially for the event, comparing it to the completely unrecognisable field that it was only a few days ago. As the final artists finish their performances, the attendants slowly start to vacate the festival area. The sun starts coming up. Alex and Mila make their way to the woodcutting shed they had reserved beforehand and the intoxicated Filip disappears in a common manner, leaving me to wander the area. I meet up with Tom from sound tech, who is busy packing up his gear.

"Lev! Great show as usual!"

"It was good show. The play button worked," I tell him jokingly. "You here with the usual crew?"

"Sure. They're all packed up. We're heading out in half an hour. You need a ride back to city?"

"If you're offering."

"There's always room on the tour bus!"

I make my way to the parking lot and find the crew area, wait for Tom and hitch a ride back to the city. The sun has now risen and birds start their usual morning orchestra. On the way back we finish off a few beers he had liberated from the festival and recap the preparation of the event. He lets me know that he had trouble getting in touch with me during the week, but I quickly explain the situation and talk about the events on the island. It all worked out.

The driver drops me off in the city centre, I say my goodbyes and make my way to the gas station near my home. The 24-hour convenience store welcomes me with a familiar ring at the door and I grab the snack sausage I was looking forward to the whole week. Arriving at home, I take the elevator to the top floor and while searching for keys notice two pieces of paper in my bag. One with a social media handle and one with a phone number, simply signed "S". I unlock the door, kick off my shoes, throw my keys in the bowl by the door and make my way to the living room. The bag drops on the floor and I fall on the couch, dead tired.

I wake to the already familiar feeling of it being long past midday, dig out the work laptop from my bag and make a large cup of coffee to match the amount of work I need to get done during the day.

The next day starts unusually quietly, as if a new national holiday had been recently announced that I had never heard of. Buses empty, streets quieter than usual, but at least I got to wake up at a normal time to be somewhat alert for the duties at work. A few meetings and some paperwork along with numerous emails need my attention at the office. Before I even realise, the time is 5PM and it's time to head back home. The bus, still as empty as before, takes me to my stop. I step off the transport, now just a five minute walk from home, again greeted by a sprinkle of spring rain. I stand in place and take a moment to acclimate, to get back in the mindset of weekly work. I look around, but there's nobody calling my name this time to offer me a ride. Making my way home, I once again stop by the gas station for a motivational snack and quick drink. The road home takes me through a park, past numerous tall apartment buildings and an old stadium that is already being demolished for constructing a fresh office complex. Home is now in sight. I turn the last corner and spot a car parked diagonally in front of the entrance to the building. I approach the car and the idiot responsible for the manoeuvre sitting on the hood, smoking a cigarette.

"So, Lev. Round two?" he asks, blowing a big puff of smoke.

"Really? What took you so long?" I say excitedly. We shake hands. I throw my work bag in the trunk and get in the passenger seat of the silver station wagon.

"There's a festival at Diagonov in four days. We thought of dropping by," he says as he sits in the car.

"We?"

He points behind him. "Me and some people," he replies nonchalantly.

I look behind, surprised to find S and M sitting in the back seat, smiling. I look back at the driver. "Diagonov is three thousand kilometres away. I'm not sure your Silver Shadow will survive the trip, even if we do. You brought your toolkit?"

"We will find a way." He starts up the car and shifts it into gear. We are on our way.

It's a Monday.

Contents:

Printed in Great Britain
by Amazon